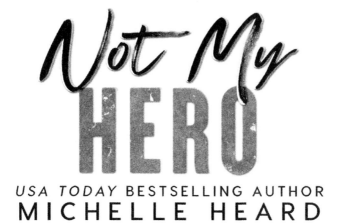

USA TODAY BESTSELLING AUTHOR
MICHELLE HEARD

Cover Designer: Lori LovesBooks Jackson

Cover Model: Ben Sellect

Photographer Credit: Wander Book Club Photography

TABLE OF CONTENTS

Dedication

For the silent ones.

Songlist

Spotify – Not My Hero by Michelle Heard

Synopsis

He walked into school on his first day and didn't care what the other students thought of him.

Dark. Broody. Dangerous.

He didn't care where I cared too much.
Then the rumors started.
He failed his senior year at his previous school. His brother committed suicide. It's his fault.

And for one blessed week, I wasn't the topic of discussion.

You see, I'm the daughter of a socialite who has no soul. I'm the one paying for her sins. They never let me forget where I come from, and she never stops telling me what a failure I am.

But then Colton Lawson looks at me, and unlike the other students, his dark gaze seems to see through the dark lies spun around me.

He starts appearing out of nowhere, fighting my battles for me only to stalk away, making me feel like I'm nothing but a nuisance.

My name is Brie Weinstock, and this is my story of how a boy walked into my hell and fought for me, even though I never expected him to.

The question is, am I strong enough to repay the favor?

Not My Hero

A Standalone, full-length novel in
The Black Mountain Academy Series
*(A Spin-off from Trinity Acadamy & Coldhearted
Heir.)*

Young Adult / High School Romance.
This book deals with sensitive subjects of abuse.

*"Don't let the noise of other's opinions drown
out your own inner voice."* **— Steve Jobs.**

Family Tree

COLTON LAWSON

↓

Brady Lawson

Brother
(Brady was Jade's boyfriend in Coldhearted Heir)

BRIE WEINSTOCK

↓

Serena Weinstock
Mother
(Villain in the Trinity Academy Series)

Chapter 1

BRIE

When I was younger, I used to pretend I was an alien. I dreamt my family would come and get me and take me back to a world where I would fit in. Or I'd get powers once I turned sixteen. Like in the movie I Am Number Four. Nothing huge. Just being invisible would've been great.

But sixteen came and went. I'll be eighteen soon and have pretty much given up on dreaming about things that will never happen.

Still, I can't complain. I got my wish. Kind of. Most people don't notice me. They just pass by me as if I don't exist.

If only everyone would ignore me.

Taking a deep breath, I walk into the school, aka the pits of hell, to start my senior year. Black Mountain Academy is supposed to be a private school for the elite, but it's the same as any other school where the bullies rule and the teachers turn a blind eye.

I used to attend church until I learned hell was a place where your worst nightmares came true. I figured, seeing as I'm already there, I shouldn't have to bother with walking the straight and narrow.

Keeping my head low, I make my way over to my locker. When I have it open, I huddle closer and hide behind the door.

"Look, fresh meat," a girl whispers behind me.

I don't glance at the new student because there's always a handful every year. They'll somehow fit in with the other students. It always boggles my mind. How other people can just fit in while I remain an outcast.

Taking a clean uniform from the bag I always carry around with me, I place the clothes in my locker. I've learned the hard way to keep extra clothes at school.

Someone bumps hard into my back, and it slams my body against the locker. "Whoops," I hear Sully, one of the biggest bullies in school, laugh. "Didn't see you there."

My muscles grow tense, and I quickly slam the locker shut. I grip hold of the strap over my shoulder, and hunching forward, I attempt to make myself smaller.

"Hey now," Sully chuckles. He slams his hand against the metal and blocks my escape. Crowding my personal space, he pinches some of my hair between his forefinger and thumb. "Did you miss me, Weinstock?"

I swallow hard, clutching the strap tighter until my fingers turn white. Sully's the most arrogant person I know. He thinks he's god's gift to women, and it doesn't help that he's always surrounded by a bunch of girls.

He leans down, then whispers, "I sure as fuck missed you."

A commotion of whispers sounds up, and luckily it draws Sully's attention away from me. Using the distraction to my advantage, I rush down the hallway. Before I round the corner, I glance back to make sure Sully's not following me, and that's when I see what the eager whispers are about.

A new boy. Dark hair and dark eyes. He looks downright scary. Anger's etched hard into his features, and the nose ring and earrings make him look dangerous. He's taller than most of the other boys, and the way he walks makes it look like he's prowling for his next victim.

Which will probably be me.

I disappear around the corner and slip into my English class. At the beginning of the new school year, I always try to be first, so I can get the desk in the corner. I sit down and dig in my bag for my sketchpad. Pulling out a pencil, I open the page I'm busy on, and then I stare at the drawing. I'm working on a shadow image of a woman wading through a shallow lake.

When other students start to trickle into class, I begin to shade the shadowy parts darker.

Someone bumps against my desk, and years of training have my hand hovering over the picture, so I don't accidentally draw a line through it.

"What the fuck are you drawing?" Michael asks. Just hearing his voice has the hairs on my body rising. Michael Jones is trouble in the worst way. I'd rather face a hundred Sullys before having to deal with Michael. I've heard rumors he raped a girl from a neighboring school, and since then, I've done my best to stay out of his way.

Michael places his hand on my shoulder, and his fingers dig into my collarbone until it starts to throb. "Damn, bitch, that looks pretty fucked up. You're a crazy one, aren't you?" He leans down, and my body begins to tremble from all the effort it's taking to sit still.

I want to get up and run. I want to run to the ends of the earth until I no longer have breath in my lungs. And then I want to jump into oblivion.

I feel Michael's breath on my ear, and it fills me with revulsion. "I have a thing for girls who are into kinky shit, so I might make an exception for you."

I shut my eyes tightly, sending up a silent prayer the teacher will walk into class.

"You're in my way," a harsh voice snaps.

My eyes fly open, and I peek through my hair, hanging like a curtain between the class and me.

"What you gonna do about it?" Michael sneers as he straightens to his full length, but he still has to look up at the new guy.

Michael takes a threatening step forward. "Colton Lawson, right? You're new in town. I heard you killed your brother." He lets out a low whistle. "That's some fucked up shit. Are you going to off me as well?"

My eyes dart to Colton's face. He looks like he could murder someone, and it sends shivers prickling over my skin. His eyes are like bottomless pits of darkness as he stares at Michael. Then his lips part. "Move."

Michael seldom backs down, so when he steps forward, ramming his shoulder into Colton's before he walks to the other side of the class, I'm surprised.

Colton takes the desk next to mine, and I'm acutely aware of every movement he makes. I dare a glance as he sets something down, and when I see it's *The Art of War* by *Sun Tzu*, a frown forms between my eyebrows.

He doesn't look like the type that reads.

Mrs. Ramsey walks into the classroom. "Settle down."

I turn my attention back to my sketch and focus on shading it darker.

"We'll be reading *How To Kill A Mockingbird* this year." A hand appears in my line of sight, and without a word, Mrs. Ramsey closes my sketchpad before placing the assigned book on top of it.

She stops at Colton's desk and picks up the paperback on his desk. "Is this what you're currently reading?"

"Yes." His answer is short, making it sound like he's annoyed.

"It's an excellent read. I'd like to hear your thoughts on it once you're done."

Colton doesn't reply, and as Mrs. Ramsey continues up the aisle, I dare a glance in his direction.

I watch as he thumbs through his copy of *How To Kill A Mockingbird*. His hands seem strong, and veins snake up his forearms.

My gaze keeps sneaking upward until it collides with his dark eyes. Instantly, my head snaps down, and I stare wide-eyed at the cover in front of me.

Crap! I know better than to draw attention to myself.

Feeling overly self-conscious, I ball my hands into tight fists on my lap.

The lesson feels like it's taking forever, and when the bell finally rings, I grab all my stuff and dart up from my chair. I'm out of the class before the other students and quickly walk to my locker. I place my copy of the English reading material in it, then stop by the restroom before hurrying to my next class.

Sometimes I feel it's all my life consists of. Running and hiding.

As I dart into the classroom, water splashes all over the front of my uniform.

"You gotta watch where you're going, Weinstock," Sully chuckles.

I know he did it on purpose, and I choose to ignore him, but then he laughs, "Oh damn, looks like someone pissed herself."

The whole class laughs, and it makes my cheeks flame with embarrassment.

For a moment, I freeze like a frightened deer, but then Mr. Matthews' voice snaps me back into action as he passes by me. "Clean up that mess and take your seat!"

I dig tissues out of my bag and quickly wipe up the puddle on the floor.

"Be glad I didn't drown you," Sully chuckles. It's a jab at what my mother did. She was once a socialite until she ruined her own life by trying to drown a fellow student at Trinity Academy. Kingsley Hunt. I wish I could meet her. I'd like to see what the girl who survived my mother looks like.

Straightening up, I throw the tissues away, then anxiously glance at the remaining open seats. The one in the corner is still available, but Colton has taken the desk next to it.

Dang.

"Sit!" Mr. Matthews snaps.

I dart forward and keep my eyes on the floor until I reach the corner desk. Taking the seat, I notice a scrap of paper, and I shove it aside. I pull the wet fabric away from my chest, hoping it will dry quickly.

I'm not good at math, and luckily Mr. Matthews doesn't pay much attention to us while he drones on. I open my art book, and I'm just about to continue with my sketch when my eyes are drawn to the scrap of paper.

Someone from the previous class probably left it here. Reaching for it, I fold it open.

'Remember, no one can make you feel inferior without your consent.' – Eleanor Roosevelt.

The quote hits like a ten-ton train, and it derails my emotions.

Yeah? Eleanor probably never had to deal with Sully or Michael, who love to torture me every chance they get.

She never had to deal with my mother, who continually reminds me I'm nothing more than an unfortunate by-product of one alcohol-induced night between her and some man. A stranger whose name she didn't even bother to get.

At least, that's one way of looking at it.

My opinion? That my mother had me because she needed someone to torture, so she could feel better about her own life that's nothing short of disastrous.

Inferior? That's not how I feel.

I just feel alone and unwanted. All my life, I've been judged for the way my mother behaves. She's a cruel woman who has a high opinion of herself. She blames the world and me for her problems. My grandparents practically exiled her to this town because she's unhinged and harmful to their public image. They also refuse to acknowledge my existence.

Letting out a sigh, I neatly fold the scrap of paper and tuck it into my bag.

COLTON

She read the quote. I watch her shove the paper into her bag, and then she continues to draw.

There's a frustrated pang in my chest. I was hoping the quote would mean something to her. I don't know, maybe enlighten her the same way it did me. But it doesn't look like the words meant anything to her.

Something about her reminds me of Brady. Just like my brother, she looks timid and scared of her own shadow.

Brady.

I shut my eyes against the grief that shudders through me. It's not as intense anymore. Three months have passed since Brady shot himself, but there are moments when it feels like it just happened. I'll suddenly smell the blood. I'll see his vacant eyes.

If I allow myself to think of everything that happened, I'll break. It feels like all it will take for me to lose my mind is one small shove.

Before Brady died, life was a constant battle. I had to fight our father because my mom and Brady wouldn't. They cowered whenever Dad flew off the rails. But I couldn't. It's like his anger triggered something inside me to keep fighting. To keep forging ahead because retreating would mean that he'd turn his rage toward them.

That night, I backed off and left because it felt like I would kill our father if I stayed at home a second longer. The one night I retreated cost me my brother's life.

If I could turn back time, I'd stay and kill our father if it meant Brady would still be here. I'd spend the rest of my life behind bars so my brother could live.

But I retreated.

I left Brady to face that monster.

The rumors are right. I did kill my brother.

Opening my eyes, I try to focus on the book I'm reading. At first, I read to escape, but now it's so much more. My father is nothing but an abusive asshole, and my mother checked out of reality the day we buried Brady.

I can't give up like Brady did. I just don't have it in me. I can't lose my shit like my mother did because then there won't be anyone to look after her. And truthfully, I'd rather die a thousand deaths before I become anything like my father.

Into Thin Air by *Jon Krakauer* taught me how to survive when staring death in the face. The book changed my life.

Since then, I've been devouring books that show the unbreakable spirit of those who have survived the unthinkable.

Where my parents have failed to teach me anything of value, books have become my guide, my perseverance, my moral compass.

The teacher begins with class, and I close my book, so I can pay attention because I sure as hell don't want to fail my senior year again.

"Psst…"

I let out a slow breath, instantly annoyed. It's the same idiot who was hurting the girl in English. I hate people like him. People like my father. They only know how to hurt – how to destroy. I've dealt with his kind all my life.

The guy waves a hand to get my attention from where he's sitting a desk up in the next row over. "Hey."

Clenching my jaw, I slant my eyes in his direction. He leans back to hand me a piece of paper. When I don't move to take it, he tosses it onto my desk. "Pass it on." He gestures to the girl next to me.

Not caring that I'll upset him, I read the note.

Couldn't help but notice you're all wet for me. Did I hit your G-spot in English?

My eyes snap back up to his, and then I tear the note into tiny pieces.

"What the fuck?" he hisses.

Taking a deep breath, I turn my gaze back to the teacher.

I have zero time for the parasites of life. If you give them half a chance, they'll suck you dry. Not that there's much left of me. Brady's death stripped all meaning from my life.

When the bell rings, I gather my stuff, and before I'm done shoving it into my bag, the girl next to me is out of her chair and rushing up the aisle. Her shoulders are hunched forward, and her black hair hangs around her like a cloak she's trying to hide behind. Her whole appearance screams at me to look away. To not notice her.

She reminds me so much of my brother, and knowing what happened to him when the pressure became too much, has me taking notice. Before Brady's suicide, I probably wouldn't have looked twice at her.

I get up, but then the parasite blocks my way. "That note was for Brie." His posture is threatening.

There are four kinds of people in life. The parasites who feed off others, aka bullies who get off on the fear they spread. The sheep who just exist, going through the same shit every day. The deers who mind their own business but then either freeze or run whenever they're threatened. And then there are the bears who are tolerant until you fuck with them.

I try my best to be the latter.

I don't bother giving him any kind of reaction and just push by him. When I step out into the hallway, the parasite bumps into me. I stop walking and clench my jaw as I turn my head in his direction.

He steps into my personal space, puffing his chest out like a damn peacock. "Do you have any idea who I am?"

I used to think I was one of the most patient people on the planet, but it turns out I was eating shit like the rest of the sheep.

No more. Not since that night.

I drop my bag to the floor, and not caring who he is, I shove the parasite hard. He staggers back, slamming against the opposite wall with a dull thud. Surprise flashes over his face before he darts forward. The moment he takes a swing at me, I duck to the side, and he ends up slamming his fist into the wall.

24

"Michael!" One of the teachers snap. "Get to class. Now."

I pick up my bag, and giving Michael-the-fucking-parasite a glare, I walk to my locker.

If he knew what I survived, he'd steer clear of me. I've dealt with much worse. My father makes the likes of Michael look like a joke.

———————————

Thanks to the little show earlier with Michael, I'm the topic of discussion.

I walk toward an empty table with my lunch, and sitting down, I hear some of the students whisper.

'I heard he's psychotic. Like no emotion. That's freaky weird.'

'I saw the fight with Michael, and I shit you not, he was cold as ice.'

'I think it's hot.'

'Yeah? So was Ted Bundy.'

I'm not here to make an impression and couldn't be bothered with what the other students think of me. I'm here to finish school so I can get a job. Right now, we're living off the money Mom gets from my father, and I don't like it one bit. Once I start working, I'll take care of us, and my father can shove his money up his ass.

That's the only goal I have for this year. Just to get through it.

Taking a bite of the meatloaf, I let my gaze drift over the nearby tables until it stops on the one where the girl, Brie, is sitting.

Half the day has passed, and I haven't seen her smile once.

I take another bite of the food while a frown forms on my forehead.

She's the first person that has caught my attention since we moved to this town three months ago.

Maybe it's because of the flash of fear I saw on her face when I caught her staring at me. I didn't like that one bit. I know how erosive fear is, and I'll be damned before making another person feel that way.

Maybe, just maybe, I can do for her what I couldn't do for Brady.

Is it even possible to redeem myself?

Chapter 2

BRIE

Sitting across from Aspen, I stare at the meatloaf that looks unappetizing. Aspen is the student body president and really a nice girl. She's the closest thing I have to a friend. We spend our lunches together, eating in silence. It's the way I prefer it.

Life has taught me that words are meaningless. Since I can remember, I've always been silenced, and the few times I tried to speak up for myself were disastrous.

So now I just keep quiet.

"How was your holiday break?" Aspen asks.

I keep my eyes on my plate as I lie, "Fine."

The past three months were nothing short of hell. As much as I hate school, I'd rather face Sully, Michael, and all the other bullies than being stuck with my mother.

Aspen twirls her spaghetti around her fork, and it makes me wish I had opted for that instead of the meatloaf. Sully was behind me in line, so I grabbed the first thing I could to get away from him.

"You should join the student council," Aspen states as if it's even an option. She might be an outcast like me, but she's feisty and an achiever.

Me? Not so much.

Actually, not at all.

I shake my head, and it draws a sigh from Aspen. She brings her water bottle to her mouth but pauses to mutter, "I swear it's not as bad as you th–" Her words cut off when my eyes widen on Knox and a girl that's practically trying to become one with his arm. Both are bad news, and I duck my head down low as they come up behind Aspen.

I hear Aspen snap, "What do you want, Knox?"

"Be at my Jeep at three," he growls, and just the tone of his voice is enough to make fear ripple over me.

"No can do," Aspen replies, sounding careless and not as if she's facing off with Knox, one of the biggest bullies at the academy. "I have a student council meeting after school."

I wish I had her courage.

"Of course you fucking do," Knox barks, and the threatening edge to his words makes my stomach knot into a tense bundle.

The girl on Knox's arm mutters, "Nice pearls, prude."

"Isn't it time for you to go back to your coffin, Morticia?" Aspen retorts, and it makes the corner of my mouth twitch.

I hear the other girl snarl and dare a quick peek because I need to know when I should make a run for it. The last thing I have strength for is to get stuck in a fight that has nothing to do with me. Especially with Knox. He's bad news with a capital B. There are rumors that he killed his mother. I don't know if they're true, but whenever I've gotten in his way, he has never hesitated to shove me aside like I'm nothing more than trash.

Aspen makes a cross with her fingers. "May the power of Christ compel you." There's so much bravery on her face, I can't help but stare while some of the other students snicker.

But then Knox stalks back to our table, and picking up Aspen's plate of spaghetti, he dumps it over her head.

I cringe away, knowing what it feels like. My cheeks flame up with mortification on Aspen's behalf as the other students burst out in laughter.

Aspen picks at a couple of strands of spaghetti, then mutters, "Asshole."

There's a sneer around Knox's mouth that makes him look treacherous. "I suggest you stop running your mouth, Stray." He grabs hold of Aspen's chin, forcing her to look up at him. "Or it will get a lot worse. Trust me."

Stop, Aspen. Don't bate him any further.

Luckily she doesn't, and once Knox walks away with the girl, I force a sympathetic smile to my face. I know too well what it feels like to be bullied and hate that it just happened to Aspen.

"Let's go to the bathroom so you can clean up," I offer.

I might not interact with people a lot, but Aspen has only been nice to me. Also, I've had so much experience with cleaning up that it's second nature to me.

And then there's the real reason – so I can get out of the cafeteria before someone decides to pick on me.

COLTON

As the day progresses, I hear more rumors about me spreading like wildfire.

The bottom line is half the school thinks I'm broody and full of shit, while the other half thinks I'm dangerous and that it's my fault my brother is dead.

Little do they know I just want to be left alone, so I can finish this year. I'm not here to make friends, and I'm definitely not interested in being popular. I'm hoping they'll find something new to talk about by the end of the week.

Walking into the last class for the day, I see Brie sitting in the corner, which means I share five classes with her.

I take the seat next to her and notice she's working on a new sketch.

Once everyone is seated, the teacher begins to talk. He pretty much says the same thing as the rest of the teachers, then scribbles his name on the board. Mr. Donati.

"For your first assignment…" Mr. Donati grins as the class groans. "I want you each to tell me why you chose this class. A short paper, two thousand words. And I want it done by tomorrow when you walk through that door." He locks eyes with a girl that was last to arrive. "On time."

Mr. Donati starts with the lesson, and my eyes drift over to the sketch Brie is working on. The movement of her hand as she draws is hypnotizing, and I zone out.

I watch as the image takes shape, and soon, there's a frown etched onto my face. Brie's drawing a girl that's screaming while gripping her hair. She's really good because I can actually feel the emotions jumping off the page. Frustration and torment.

Is that how she feels?

When the bell rings, I'm ripped out of the reverie I was caught in. Brie again rushes out of the class, and after I've packed my own things, I get up and leave.

There's no sign of Brie as I head out of the building. When I get to my truck, I throw my bag on the passenger seat before sliding in behind the wheel. I steer the vehicle carefully out of the parking area, but it takes a couple of minutes because everyone is in a hurry to get away from school.

Once I'm finally driving down the main road toward the neighborhood I live in, I spot Brie walking. For a moment, I contemplate stopping to offer her a ride but then decide it would be weird, seeing as we don't know each other.

She probably doesn't even know my name.

Getting home and pulling up the driveway, I notice the lawn needs some care. I'll mow it once it's cooler outside.

Walking into the house, that's similar to the one we had in California, silence greets me.

My father has been throwing money at my mother in the hopes he can buy her back.

God, I hope she doesn't give in. There's no way I'll ever let that man back into my life.

I kick off my shoes at the front door, and taking the stairs to the second floor, I head to my mother's room. Softly nudging the door open, I see Mom lying on the bed.

Brady's death broke her. Right after his suicide, she went into overdrive, rushing to get me away from my father. Once Mom had us settled in the town where she grew up, and she knew I was safe, it's like she just shut down.

She hardly leaves the house and spends most of her time in bed. I take care of the shopping, cooking, and... practically everything.

I move closer, and sitting down on the bed, I place my hand on her shoulder. "I'm home."

She turns her face to me, her eyes dimmed of all light and an exhausted expression, making her look years older than she is. "Did you have a good first day?"

I lie down behind her and wrap my arm around her. "It was okay. The teachers seem nice. I got a ton of homework."

"Want to order something for dinner?" she whispers as if it would take too much energy to speak a little louder.

"I'll make us something," I reply. I give her a hug and press a kiss to the side of her head. "Want me to bring you something to drink."

She shakes her head and burying her face in her pillow, she grips my arm and pulls me closer. "Can you just stay with me a little while?"

I snuggle back down and begin to talk about the first thing that comes to my mind. "There's a girl at school. Her name is Brie."

"Yeah?" Mom's voice cracks over the single word.

"She draws really well."

I don't know why I'm bringing up Brie.

"I'm glad you're making friends," Mom mumbles.

I don't correct her. The last thing I want is to worry my mother unnecessarily.

I stay with Mom for a couple of minutes longer, then say, "I'm going to get started with my homework."

She nods. "Let me know if you need help with anything."

"Sure." I won't, though. I do my best to be the strong one so Mom can just heal.

I give her one last squeeze, then get up and go to my own room. I sit down and open my laptop, deciding to work on the essay Mr. Donati gave us.

Why did I choose history?

Cause it's easy, and I just want to pass my senior year so I can look after my mother.

I begin to type, explaining it in detail. He'll either give me an A or ask the counselor to meet with me. Either way, I'm not going to lie.

My entire life has been built on lies. My future sure as hell won't be.

After two hours of working on the essay, I stretch out to loosen my muscles. I go to change into a pair of sweatpants and a t-shirt and slip on my sneakers. Heading out to the backyard, I pull the lawnmower out of the shed.

The sun is setting by the time I'm done mowing the lawn. Walking back to the house, I pull my t-shirt off and use it to wipe the sweat from my face and back of my neck. I grab a bottle of water from the fridge and chug it down as I go to throw the shirt in the laundry basket.

I kick off the sneakers and get a fresh shirt to pull on, then head back to the kitchen.

I take two steaks from the freezer and put them in some hot water so they can thaw, thinking I should've taken them out earlier.

I've gotten used to cooking for us. It's either that or take-out, and I can't stomach junk food anymore.

My thoughts go back to school while I prepare dinner. None of the students stood out. Well, except for Brie. The rest are the same as at my previous school.

I wonder what Brie's story is. Is she just an introvert, or is there more?

From experience, I know how easy it is to hide abuse. God, you do everything in your power so people won't find out.

We didn't lie so my father wouldn't get in trouble. We did it so people wouldn't pity us.

Fuck, if only I had said something. If only I'd done more.

Then Brady would still be here.

When the food is ready, I prepare a plate for Mom. Grabbing a bottle of water and cutlery, I set it all on a tray. I carry the meal to her room and say, "Time to eat."

She lets out a groan.

"Come on. I tried something new with the steak. I grilled it in butter and garlic."

Mom sits up and wipes the hair out of her face. I set the tray down and whisper, "It would really make me happy if you eat half of it at least."

It's a low blow, but if I don't guilt-trip her, she doesn't eat.

I wait for her to take a bite of the steak. Mom gives me a weak smile. "My son, the chef. It's delicious."

Pleased that she's eating, I go grab the book I'm reading and walk back to the kitchen. Taking my plate, I go sit outside on the porch.

Eating, I stare out over the lawn. I spent the summer planting shrubs and flowers. Mom always loved gardening, and I hoped it would draw her out of the house. But it didn't.

When I'm finished with the meal, I read for a while before I go back inside to clean the kitchen. Grabbing the tray from Mom's room, I smile when I see that she ate most of the food.

"It was really good," she murmurs, "Thank you, sweetheart."

"You're welcome." I finish the chores then settle in at my desk to continue with my homework.

Our life here is a total contrast to how things were in California. There's no noise. No rages. No demoralizing words. No beatings. Just silence.

It's peaceful, and I know Brady would've loved it here.

If only we had moved sooner.

Chapter 3

BRIE

I managed to sneak into the house without my mom realizing I'm home from school.

Even though I have a laptop, I prefer to write by hand. Once I'm done with my essay for history, a smile tugs at my lips. My stomach growls, and I rub a hand absentmindedly over it. I should've eaten the meatloaf at lunch.

Glass breaks somewhere in the house, and it makes my head snap up from where I'm reading over what I wrote.

"Brie!" Mom's voice is shrill as it echoes through the house.

My shoulders slump, and getting up, I sigh. At least I managed to avoid her for a couple of hours.

Leaving my room, my steps feel heavy as I go down to the kitchen. I find my mother staring at the pieces of what used to be a cocktail glass.

Crouching by the mess, I begin to pick up the largest pieces.

My mother doesn't move, and I can feel her eyes burning on the top of my head. "They must've swapped you at birth." My heart kicks against my ribs, and I work faster. "I'm sure I can sue them for negligence."

It's not the first time I've heard the words. Where my mother has ginger hair, I have black. She has green eyes, and I have blue. I look nothing like her.

Her perfectly manicured hand reaches for my face, and a long nail digs in under my chin as she forces me to look up at her. "God only knows who's kid you are. Not mine, that's for sure." Her sharp gaze moves over my features. "You're so... dull. Would it kill you to try harder? What will it take to light a fire under you? Huh?"

I stand up and shuffle backward to put some space between us, then mumble, "I'll try harder."

"No fight at all," she sneers. I turn to throw the shards of glass away, but then she grabs hold of my arm, yanking me back so I'll face her. "I'm not done talking to you."

I swallow hard. "Sorry."

"I'm sure the whole town is talking about the bastard kid that's living with me."

I lower my eyes to the remaining mess on the floor.

The flat of her hand connects with the side of my head. "Show some life! You're like a goddamn zombie."

The shock of the slap vibrates through my body, and I draw my bottom lip between my teeth in an attempt to fight for control over my emotions. I want to lash out. I want to fight back. But no good will come from it. It will only enrage her more, which will mean more trouble for me.

She grabs hold of my left hand, and a shard of glass tumbles to the floor. She forces my fingers to close over the pieces and then begins to squeeze. "Nothing?" She tightens her grip around my fist. Sharp splinters of pain cut through my skin. "Seriously? What will it take to get a reaction from you?"

Blood trickles over the sides of my palm, and I watch as it drips to the floor.

When she lets go of my hand, I let out a slow breath. She shoves me hard, and I stumble before I fall down. Somehow, I managed to keep hold of the glass pieces, but the sudden movement makes them cut deeper.

"Clean up," she snaps.

I don't move and wait for her to pour the cosmopolitan into a new cocktail glass. As she saunters out of the kitchen, I hear her say, "I can't believe I'm stuck with Kingsley's lookalike. I should dye your hair and get you contacts to wear. Maybe if you look more like me and less like that bitch you'll grow a backbone."

I wait until she's gone before I climb to my feet. Walking over to the trashcan, I gingerly pick the shards from my hand. When I rinse the blood off in the sink, I shut my eyes as the cuts burn.

At least it's not my right hand. I can still draw, and that's really all that matters.

I wrap a piece of paper towel around my palm and fingers, then wipe up the mess on the floor before I go to my bathroom, where I keep a first aid kit.

I clean the cuts as best as I can, then wrap a bandage around my hand. Wanting to finish my homework so I can climb in bed, I go sit at my desk and read through the essay one last time. I move it to the side and pull my English book closer.

"I've made an appointment for you at the hairdresser tomorrow to get your damn hair colored," Mom suddenly says.

I didn't hear her come in and caught off guard, I instantly dart up and move to the side.

She glances down at my school work and shakes her head. My heart drops to my feet when she picks up the essay I just spent hours working on.

With a sigh, she says, "It's such a waste of money to have you in that private school." She crumples the papers, her eyes boring spitefully into mine, daring me to challenge her, and my body jerks in an immediate reflex to save my essay. But my survival instinct wins out, and my shoulders slump.

She lets out a disappointed sigh as she drops my crumpled assignment to the floor. "Such a waste of... everything really."

As soon as she's out of my room, I rush to shut the door, wishing I had a key to lock it. Hurrying back to my essay, I pick it up and do my best to straighten the papers. I bite my bottom lip to keep from crying as misery weighs heavily down on me.

Just one year. Hopefully, I'll get accepted to an art school, so I can get out of here.

Hopefully.

———————————

Things are weird at school. The day is almost over, and no one has picked on me. There were no snide comments about me or my mother. Not that I'm complaining. The reprieve is welcome, especially after last night.

During art class, I work to finish the sketch I started yesterday. When it's completed, I sit back and stare at the self-portrait. Yesterday, Miss Snow told us we could use any form of art as long as the work represented us. Now that I'm done with mine, I feel apprehensive about showing her.

I glance around at the other students to see how far they are and whether I have time to draw something else.

"What's wrong, Brie?" Miss Snow asks, and as she moves in my direction, I quickly close my sketchpad.

"Ahh… nothing," I mumble.

Crap.

She stops by me and reaches for my sketchpad.

"I'm not done yet," I try to stop her, but she opens the book and thumbs through the two pages I've drawn on.

My eyes anxiously dart between her face and my sketchpad, and I almost wring my hands, but the painful cuts under the bandange stop me.

Emotions flash over her features, and then her eyebrows draw together. When her gaze moves to me, I quickly look down. Her hand settles on my shoulder as she places the book down in front of me. I smell her soft perfume as she crouches next to me.

44

"Please stay after class. You're talented, and I'd like to talk to you about your options for college."

Not what I expected. I let out the breath I was holding and nod.

I thought she was either going to lay into me for drawing depressing stuff or ask me to see the counselor, which would be a total waste of time.

"In the meanwhile, can you draw a representation of yourself five years from now?"

She rises to her feet and repeats the assignment for the rest of the class to hear.

Five years from now.

I open to a clean page and take hold of a pencil. Staring at the blank canvas, I wonder what my life would be like in the future.

Will I still have contact with my mother?

Probably not.

There won't be any Sullys and Michaels.

Hopefully.

The corner of my mouth lifts slightly as I begin to sketch. I imagine myself standing with my face raised to the sun and hundreds of tiny butterflies flying around me.

Five years from now, I'll be hopeful and free.

When the bell rings, I let out a disappointed huff. I wish I could spend all my time in art. I pack up and wait for the other students to clear out before I walk to Miss Snow's desk.

She gestures to a chair. "Bring it closer and sit down."

I move it closer and take a seat. Miss Snow smiles at me, and it eases the tension a little.

"You're quite expressive in your sketches," she begins. I fist the fabric of my skirt with my right hand. "Have you thought about college?"

I nod. "I'm going to apply to a couple of art schools."

"If you continue to deliver such good work, I'll definitely write you a recommendation letter."

A smile graces my lips. "Really?"

"Of course." Her smile softens, and she leans a little forward. "Is everything okay at home?"

The smile falls from my face, and the word bursts from me, "Yes."

Miss Snow places her hand over mine and gives it a squeeze, but it only makes me feel uncomfortable. "If you need to talk to someone, you can always come to me."

I nod, all my muscles tensing. I wet my lips and getting up, I hoist my bag over my shoulder. "I should go. I'm late for history."

"Let me write you a note, so you don't get in trouble." She scribbles onto a piece of paper and holds it out to me. When I take hold of it, Miss Snow says, "I'm looking forward to seeing what you draw next."

I nod again before I quickly walk out into the hallway. I slip into the classroom and hand Mr. Donati the note from Miss Snow.

He reads it, then asks, "Where's your essay?"

I dig it out of my bag and cringe with shame when I hand him the wrinkled papers.

"What? Did the dog try to eat it?" he asks, and it makes the class snicker.

I can feel my face turning red as I shake my head. "My mother thought it was trash. I can rewrite it. I just didn't want you to think I didn't do it."

"It's fine. Sit."

I rush to my seat and notice another scrap of paper lying on the desk. Only when Mr. Donati continues with the lesson do I open it.

'Too many of us are not living our dreams because we are living our fears.' – Les Brown.

I frown as I reread it.

Did someone leave this for me?

"Isn't that right, Brie?" Mr. Donati suddenly says as he walks down the aisle.

"Huh?"

My eyes grow wide when he takes the paper from my hand and reads it out loud. Thank God it's just a quote, but the class still laughs.

My face reddens to the point that it feels like I could go up in flames from everyone's attention being on me.

Mr. Donati sets the paper down and taps my desk. "Focus on the lesson."

"Yes, Sir." I sit frozen with my eyes glued to the desk.

———————————

COLTON

Well, that backfired. I didn't mean to get Brie in trouble.

My eyes are drawn to the bandage around her left hand. I noticed it during English. Again, I wonder what happened.

Brie doesn't move a muscle, and as the minutes pass by, the tension coming off of her gets to me until I'm clenching my jaw.

Today has been a shitty day with Michael trying to start a fight because I bruised his ego yesterday. Also, the rest of the school is continually gossiping. They don't even bother whispering anymore.

A couple of guys were friendly during lunch, asking if I played any sports, but the second I said no, they moved onto the other new guys.

When the bell rings, I feel the tension ease as Brie darts up and runs out of the class. I let out a breath and pack my bag.

Walking into the hallway, a girl pushes away from where she was leaning against the wall. "Colton, right?"

"Yeah," I grumble. I keep walking, and she has to move to keep up.

"A bunch of us are going to Devil's Bluff. Wanna come?"

"No." I quicken my pace to get away from her.

"Your loss," she calls after me.

I feel the curious stares on me as I walk to my truck. Once I climb into the cab, I let out a sigh. I start the engine and steer the vehicle through the bustling after-school madness.

Driving down the main road, I see Brie again, and I wonder where she lives. She's walking fast with her arms crossed over her chest and her shoulders hunched forward as if she's bracing for a blizzard or something.

I glance at her one last time through the rearview mirror before I focus my gaze on the road ahead.

When I get home, I kick off my shoes at the front door and drop my bag in my room. Changing into a pair of shorts and a t-shirt, I go check on my mother.

I'm quiet as I enter her room, and when I sit down on the bed, she glances up at me. A slight smile graces her lips. "Hey, how was school?"

I lie down and hug her. "It was okay. Nothing spectacular."

"Do you have a lot of homework?" she asks, and the fact that she still shows an interest in my life gives me hope that she'll be back to her old self… one day.

"Yeah, but I first want to pull the weeds from the flower beds. Do you want to sit on the porch and keep me company?"

She shakes her head. "Another time."

Getting up, I suppress a sigh. I walk to the kitchen and grab a bag, then head out to the front. Crouching by a flower bed, I begin to pull the weeds out. The work keeps my mind busy until I'm breathless. I sit back and rest my forearms on my knees. I glance over the area I still have to do, and movement catches my eye.

Climbing to my feet, I'm surprised when I see Brie walking by my house. Curious where she's heading, I wait until she's passed by before I take a short cut through the flower bed. I stay a safe distance behind her so she won't notice me.

A few houses from mine, she stops in a driveway and stares at the house.

Does she live there?

Fuck she walks far. Should I offer her a ride?

She pulls a phone from her pocket and stares at it before glancing back to the house. When she turns around, my heart almost stops, and I duck behind a row of hedges.

The next moment, Brie rushes past me. I step forward and peek around the leaves. She keeps glancing behind her and then breaks out in a run.

What the hell?

Did she see me?

When she's out of sight, I walk back to my own house, and distracted by Brie's weird behavior, I finish plucking all the weeds out.

After I'm done, I take a shower to clean all the sweat and sand off. Dressed in sweatpants and a fresh shirt, I sit down to do my homework until it's time to prepare dinner.

By nine o'clock, all the chores are done, and I feel restless. I slip on my sneakers, thinking a run around the block might tire me enough to sleep.

I don't bother telling Mom I'm heading out because she won't even notice I'm gone.

Starting with a slow jog to warm up first, I glance at the houses as I pass them. Nearing the one Brie was staring at, I slow down and stop by the driveway. My gaze is drawn to the light shining from a bedroom on the second floor. With the curtains open, I have a clear view inside.

A girl comes into view, and the corner of my mouth lifts slightly. She shuts the door and turns toward the window. The smile on my face grows.

So Brie does live here.

With my eyes on her, I walk a little closer to the house. I watch as she brushes her long black hair, and it's hypnotic, just like when she draws.

Suddenly, her head snaps toward the door, and I watch as a woman walks into the room. Brie cowers away from her, and when the woman starts to yell at her, waving her hands angrily, tension winds tightly in my chest.

Brie staggers backward until her back is pressed up against the window.

The breath is knocked from my lungs when the woman lunges forward. She grabs Brie's arm and shoves her to the floor.

Without thinking it through, I run to the front door and pound a fist against the wood. My heart is hammering against my ribs, forcing the breaths to rush over my lips.

Finally, the woman, who I saw in Brie's room, opens the door, her hand fluttering over her ginger hair in an attempt to compose herself.

"Can I help you?" she asks, and even though she's breathless, she still manages to sound sugary sweet.

The atmosphere pours from the house. It's explosive and hostile.

"I'm here for Brie."

"Oh." She eyes me up and down, and I know the earrings and nose ring don't make a good impression. That's why I got them. It keeps people at a distance. "It's late," she states, the look of disapproval on her face making it clear I'm unwelcome.

"I need to ask her something about school," I lie. My eyes keep darting behind the woman. "It will only take a minute," I add. "Please."

My hands fist next to my sides as she says, "Wait here." I watch her walk deeper into the house, and then she calls, "Brie, there's someone here to see you." I watch her go up the stairs, and not able to just stand still, I move closer.

I hear the woman hiss, "Talk to the guy so he'll leave, and don't you dare tell him any of our personal business."

When I hear footsteps, I quickly dart back to the front door.

Brie's clasping her arms over her chest, and when she sees me, she anxiously glances back to where her mother is following right behind her.

This feels too familiar.

The tension and fear coming from Brie sends my blood racing through my veins. My muscles tense, and I clench my jaw to keep from responding the way I would've with my own father.

"Hey." I gesture to the bench on the porch. "Can we talk?"

She glances back at her mother, and the woman warns, "It's late. Don't be long."

Brie steps out of the house and gives me a questioning glance before she turns her gaze to the floor. "Why are you here?" she whispers.

I see the red handprint on Brie's arm that she's trying to cover, and my hands itch to grab her and run.

Like I should've done with Brady.

Just fucking run away from all of this.

"Are you okay?"

Stupid question, Colton. Of course, she's not.

Brie nods, shooting another glance toward the front door.

I see her mother's shadow fall onto the porch, and knowing she's listening, I ask, "I wanted to check if we got homework for history."

Brie's eyes fly to mine before focusing on her feet again. "No, it was just the essay we handed in today."

I step closer to her, but it only makes her tense up even more. "Can we exchange numbers? That way, I can just call next time." I say, then quickly add, "Or you can call if you need anything."

Like, help if you're being abused.

"You want my number?" she asks, sounding guarded.

"Yes." I pull my phone out of my pocket and hold it out to her. "Just type it in."

"Hurry up," her mother calls.

Brie quickly takes my phone and adds her number. When she hands the device back to me, I press dial.

"I just called you, so you'll have mine."

Brie glances at the front door, where her mother is hovering. "I should go inside."

Fuck, what do I do?

Do I just leave?

I follow after her, and once her mother comes into view, I lock eyes with the woman while saying, "I'll see you at school tomorrow, Brie."

"Okay," Brie murmurs before disappearing into the house.

I keep my eyes on the woman's, hoping to all that's holy she can read between the lines.

I know. I fucking know.

She begins to shut the door, and unable to stop myself, I step forward. Placing my hand against the wood, I stop her. My voice is a low rumble of warning, "I saw what you did."

For a moment, surprise widens her eyes, but then they narrow on me while a sneer pulls at her mouth. She leans forward and hisses, "And? What are you going to do?" She lets out a chuckle then slams the door shut.

My body begins to tremble with anger as I whisper, "I'm going to help Brie."

Chapter 4

BRIE

Cleaning my room, my movements are frantic while my eyes keep darting to the door.

She's going to be so angry!

The lump in my throat grows impossibly big, and a strangled sound escapes as I suck in a painful breath. My body trembles so severely, I keep dropping things.

A terrified breath shudders over my dry lips.

I can't believe Colton was here.

Like things weren't bad enough. How did he even know where I lived?

She's going to freak out.

I don't have time to wonder about his sudden appearance or what trouble it caused me because my mother slams my door open. My heart sets off at a maddening pace.

There's a cruel sneer around her lips as her eyes lock on me, then she snaps, "Who was that?"

"Just a boy…" I sputter. "From school."

She stalks closer until her breaths waft over my face. "He's trash. I won't have you slander my name by screwing someone like him."

My body trembles, and I'm filled with desperate anguish. I squeeze my eyes shut and draw a little back, but it only makes her grab hold of my arm.

Her nails dig into my skin as she hisses, "That boy better not come here again, or they'll find you at the bottom of Devil's Bluff."

My chin begins to tremble from holding back the tears. I bite my bottom lip hard and nod.

"You hear me!" she shouts. "Make sure he stays away."

"I-I… will," I stammer, beside myself with fear.

Letting go of my arm, she walks back to the door. Absentmindedly, I rub over my arm where it hurts.

She glances back at me, a cruel gleam in her eyes. "The next time you shower for longer than five minutes, I'll drown you."

I cower a step back.

She lets out a dark sounding chuckle. "Your lookalike might have survived, but I promise you, you won't. Don't push me."

"Yes, Ma'am," I whisper, just wanting her to leave.

She slams the door shut, and I wait a couple of minutes before I sink down on the edge of my bed.

The emotions from tonight gush to the surface, and no matter how hard I fight to keep them in, tears spill over my cheeks.

Why?

Why is life so hard?

Why did I get her for a mother?

I cover my mouth with my hands to smother the cry. Sinking down to the floor, I bring my knees to my chest and huddle in a small ball.

I can't do this anymore.

I don't want to live if this is all my life is ever going to be.

I just… can't.

Nothing in life is worth all this pain.

The sound of my phone pinging yanks me out of the dark pit of despair. I climb to my feet and pick up the device where it's lying next to my bed.

There's a message from an unknown number. Tapping on the screen, my lips part as I read the text.

'When you reach the end of your rope, tie a knot in it and hang on.' – Franklin D. Roosevelt.

Remember to add my number to your contact list. I meant what I said, call if you need anything. My house is number 29. Colton.

Shock shudders through me.

Holy crap, the quotes were from Colton?

I stand frozen for the longest time, reading the words again and again, but they only make confusion rattle through me.

Why would Colton message me? Or come to my house?

An awful thought creeps into the back of my mind.

Maybe he's pretending to be friendly, and once I let my guard down, he'll hurt me, just like Sully and Michael.

"Why is your light still on?" Mom yells as she walks by my room. I rush to the switch and turn off the light. Standing in the dark, I worry my bottom lip, listening to the sounds on the other side of the door. When I hear her's slam shut, I let out a relieved breath and climb in bed. I reread the message.

It's probably a prank.

It won't be the first time. During my junior year, Danny Gordon pretended to be interested in me. I fell for it, and everyone laughed at me.

I don't want to go through that again.

Walking into English, I keep my head down and grip my sketchpad tightly.

I sit down and let my long hair fall between the class and me. When I hear Colton sit down at his desk, I cringe closer to the wall.

I've been dreading this moment all morning. Usually, I'm on the lookout for Sully or Michael, but not today. Not knowing what Colton's intentions are, has my stomach knotted with nerves.

Mrs. Ramsey begins with the lesson, and I itch to work on my sketch, but not wanting to draw Colton's attention to me, I keep as still as I can.

I've been replaying last night over in my mind, and I just can't understand why he came to my house, or how he even knew where I lived.

And the quotes? Do they have a double meaning I'm missing? Are they threats?

I need to read them again. My knee starts to jump under the table as the minutes slowly tick by. When the bell finally rings, my nerves are shredded.

I grab my stuff and run out of the class. I dart into the nearest restroom and hide in the first available stall.

I dig through my bag for the two quotes, and my eyes race over the words.

Is he saying he's going to make me feel inferior? That I should fear him? I open the text, and a frown forms on my forehead.

I don't get it.

Feeling miserably apprehensive, I shove the scraps of paper back in my bag. I have to get to class. The last thing I need right now is detention for being late.

I make it in the nick of time and take my seat. Mr. Matthews begins droning on about things I'll never understand.

Math feels twice as long, and after getting next to no sleep last night and all the worry, it's hard to keep my eyes open. I rest my forehead on the palm of my hand and spend the entire lesson alternating between dozing off and jerking awake.

A hand shakes my shoulder, and my eyes fly open. I dart up and squeeze my body against the wall.

"Class is over," Colton says, then he walks up the aisle.

It's only then I notice everyone is leaving. I gather my stuff while willing my heartbeat to slow down.

At this rate, I'll die of a heart attack long before I can end things myself.

COLTON

Brie's a mess, and it makes me worry that I made things worse for her at home.

The way she reacted when I woke her after math has been haunting me all day long. Growing up with an abusive father, I've felt my fair share of fear and saw it living in Brady's eyes every day, but the look on Brie's face... that was something else.

When I take my seat in history, I tear a page from my notebook and write the math homework down for Brie, in case she didn't get it. Folding the paper in half, I stretch over and place it on Brie's desk.

Her eyes dart to me for a split-second before they turn to the paper, staring at it as if it's a snake. She sucks in a deep breath then reads it. A frown forms on her forehead, and she seems confused.

Maybe she struggles with math?

Mr. Donati walks down the aisle, dropping the graded papers on our desks. When he gets to mine, he says, "Great essay, Colton. Come see me after class."

I expected as much. I nod, and when he moves on to the next aisle, I glance at the A+ in bold red at the top of the paper, but it offers me no satisfaction.

An A+ for the hell I went through.

A bitter sigh escapes my lips.

An A+ for Brady killing himself.

I'll never understand how things work in this world.

My gaze drifts over to Brie's desk, and I see she got a B- right before she slips the paper under her sketchpad.

Once Mr. Donati is done handing back all the essays, he gives us our homework for the day then starts with the lesson.

Brie's knee starts to jump under her desk, and it once again distracts me. I turn my head slightly in her direction and see that she's tense as hell. There so much anxiety pouring off of her.

I remember feeling like that, knowing the school day was at an end, and I had to go home and face *him*.

An overwhelming need to help her grows in my chest.

The bell rings, and I'm ripped back to the present. I gather my stuff and make my way to the front of the class while the other students clear out.

Mr. Donati waits until we're alone, then he takes a seat on the edge of his desk and smiles at me. I've heard the girls talking, and I'm pretty sure half the class has a crush on him.

"How are you holding up?" he asks.

"I'm fine," I give the automatic response everyone expects.

His blue eyes sharpen on me as he nods, and it gives me the impression he sees right through the lie. "My door is open any time you need to talk, Colton."

"Thanks."

I turn away to leave, but then he says, "None of that should have happened. I'm sorry it did."

His words hit so hard, I struggle to get air into my lungs. It's the first time anyone said sorry, and I didn't expect the words to hurt so much.

It's because they're from the wrong person.

I nod and rush out of the class. I need to be alone, so I can shove all the emotions back down from where they're creeping out of the darkest parts of me.

As soon as I step out of the building, someone grabs the paper out of my hand.

"What do we have here?" Michael says, an egotistical smirk plastered on his face as he begins to read my essay out loud, "I chose history because it's easy." He lets out a bark of laughter and gives me a condescending look. "Wow, I think my IQ dropped from reading that," he taunts.

The second his eyes turn back to the paper, I lunge forward. I grab the essay back, and at the same time, my fist connects with his jaw.

I do my best to avoid violence because I fucking abhor it. Still, for this parasite, I'm willing to make an exception.

Michael falls to the side from the blow and grips his jaw as he climbs back to his feet. He lets out a chuckle that sounds more like a warning. "Now you've pissed me off."

Stepping into his personal space, I growl. "I already have blood on my hands. Want me to add yours as well?" I see the hesitation creep into his eyes and spit out, "You're nothing but a joke."

Mr. Donati comes out, and I expect to be sent to the office, but instead, he snaps, "Break it up, guys. Go home."

I bump my shoulder against Michael's as I push by him and clench my jaw while I fight to regain control over the rage boiling in my chest.

Climbing into my truck, I throw my bag and the essay on the passenger seat. Slamming a hand against the steering wheel, I let out a frustrated growl.

I shouldn't have hit him. I should've kept calm.

But I lost my shit just like my father.

God, I don't want to be like him.

The taste of regret and shame is bitter in the back of my throat, and I shut my eyes as I suck in a deep breath.

I'd rather die than become a monster.

———————————

The rest of the week is tiring as fuck. Michael has zero survival instincts because the parasite keeps looking to start shit with me.

I gained another enemy because I stepped in to help Brie when a guy named Sully was giving her trouble. It's done nothing to silence the rumors. Most of the students have made up their minds that I'm a psycho, and I'll most likely end up murdering Michael or Sully as well.

Can't say I'm not tempted by the idea, but all I really want is to be left alone.

"Hey, asshole!" Sully calls from the end of the hallway.

Knowing he's probably referring to me, I grab my English book from the locker and slam the door shut.

Sully catches up to me and throws his arm around my shoulders. "How's my favorite asshole today?"

I shrug his arm off, but the guy is like a fucking tick because he nudges his shoulder against mine. "Come on, no hard feelings. Let's be friends."

Yeah, I need him as a friend as much as I need to be castrated. "Ain't gonna happen," I grumble as I walk into the classroom.

"Sure?"

I sit down and drop the book on the desk. Sully comes to stand by my desk. "Last chance."

I slant my eyes up, giving him a fuck off and die look.

He shrugs. "Your loss."

Brie sits down, and it catches Sully's attention. He begins to squeeze past the front of my desk, and knowing he's probably going to pick on her, I shove my desk forward, and it sends Sully stumbling into the chair in front of me.

The class bursts out laughing, and I lean a little forward. "Oops. My bad."

"Settle down," Mrs. Ramsey calls out.

"You're dead," Sully snarls before he walks to his desk.

"Heard that shit before," I mutter. I pull the book I'm reading from my bag. I finished The Art Of War, and I have to say, it's helped a lot in dealing with Michael and Sully.

I'm now reading Unbroken, and damn, what Louis Zamperini went through is unthinkable but also encouraging. Knowing that he survived against all odds gives me hope.

Mrs. Ramsey comes down the aisle, handing back our graded work.

She stops at my desk and looks at the book, then says, "Another good one. I have a couple I can recommend if you're interested?"

"Sure."

My reply makes her smile, then she adds, "Keep up the good work."

I haven't received much praise in my life, and it causes a foreign sensation to spread through my chest.

Chapter 5

BRIE

The past week has actually been… nice. I finally got my wish because the past couple of days, I've been invisible, and it's been amazing.

Michael, Sully, and Colton have been too busy picking fights with each other to pay any unwanted attention to me. It's been an enormous relief.

All the rumors I hear between classes are about Colton and not about me, but he doesn't seem to care at all.

I wish I could be like him and just not bother with what people do or think.

Maybe one day.

My mother left for LA yesterday to visit my grandparents. I've never met them, but I'm so grateful for the reprieve it's offered me.

But my mother will be back tomorrow.

I let out a sigh as I walk into school. I'm soaking wet from the rain pouring outside and need to get to my locker for the dry uniform so I can change before class.

My foot hooks against something, and unable to catch myself, I sprawl over the floor.

Laughter explodes around me as I scramble to sit up and make sure my skirt covers everything.

"Weinstock, you gotta watch where you're walking," Sully chuckles.

Ugh… I knew it wouldn't last.

A hand appears in my line of sight, and glancing up, I see it belongs to Colton.

Yeah, sure. I'm not falling for that trick.

With my luck, he'll yank away as soon as I reach for it. Ignoring him, I climb to my feet and straighten the wet fabric of my skirt that's clinging to my legs.

Colton picks up my bag, and apprehension bleeds into my chest. He holds it out, and as I reach for the strap, my eyes dart to his face. He glares at me and shakes his head. "Stop letting them walk all over you," he grumbles before he stalks toward Sully.

I don't stick around to hear what they have to say to each other because my face is on fire with embarrassment, and I just want to get away from them.

No one asked him to interfere, and then he makes me feel like I'm an annoyance?

His comment actually hurt. It reminds me of all the times my mother has told me to grow a spine and stop being a zombie.

If only they knew how hard it is because whenever I stood up for myself in the past, it only made them all more aggressive.

"Damn, Brie," Lindy, one of the cheerleaders, calls out, "looks like your mother tried to drown you."

Her friends snicker as I rush past them. Stopping at my locker, I quickly open it and pull the bag with dry clothes out. When I shut the door and turn to walk away, Lindy blocks my way.

Her eyes scan over me with a look of disdain. "If you ask my opinion, the likes of you shouldn't be allowed to attend Black Mountain Academy."

I didn't ask.

"I noticed a couple of new outcasts joined this year, but it doesn't look like any of them wants to be your friend. Doesn't it suck being so unpopular?"

I keep my eyes trained on the floor, and taking a step to the side, I walk around her.

Then she calls out, "I hear your mom crawled back to your grandfather to beg for more money."

"Yeah, my mom works at the bank. She said your mom is broke," one of her friends joins in.

Pin prickles of shame break out over my skin, and I walk faster to get away from the taunting.

"Once a murdering leech, always a murdering leech, I guess," Lindy continues. "Ooooh, wait," she chuckles behind me, "she tried to drown you because you're so damn morbid, right?" Laughter echoes behind me. "Can't blame her."

I dart into the restroom, and when I'm safely in a stall, I stand frozen for a moment, sucking in desperate breaths of air.

They're just words, Brie.

Yeah? But it still hurts.

COLTON

Instead of picking fights with me, Sully and Michael have turned their focus back on Brie, and it aggravates the ever-loving shit out of me.

I wish she would tell them to back off, but instead, she lets them do whatever they want.

Somehow they caught onto the fact that I'm protective of Brie, and I think they're back to targeting her to get a reaction from me. It's either that or they've given up with getting me all riled up because I don't give a fuck. I'm still trying to figure out which it is.

The reason actually doesn't make a difference because watching Brie take hit after hit only to cower away brings back a shit-ton of memories from the past.

"You fucking idiot! Why are you always in the way?" Dad hollers, and a slap echoes through the house.

Shit.

I shoot up from where I was sitting on the bed, putting on my shoes, and rush out of the room. Brady's cowering in the bathroom doorway with Dad all up in his face.

"I'm tired of your shit," Dad rages and delivers another slap to the side of Brady's head.

I dart between then, pushing my brother into the bathroom. "That's enough. We're going to be late for school," the words rush from me.

74

Dad's eyes narrow on me, and a dark frown makes him look murderous as he hisses, "What did you say?"

"Jonah, please," Mom whimpers from the side.

She reaches a trembling hand out to him, and he shoves her so hard she falls backward. "Don't fucking 'Jonah please' me! It's because you baby them that I have two gutless cowards for sons."

When he grabs hold of Mom's arm, I pull the bathroom door shut behind me so Brady will be safe, and then grab hold of Dad's shoulder. "Let go of her."

Dad swings around, and the slap to my ear stuns me for a moment. "Oh, you think you're man enough to take me on?"

I glance at Mom. "Go to your bedroom."

There's a pained look mixing with the fear in her eyes, and she hesitates.

"Go, Mom!" I shout.

Dad lets out a bark of laughter. He shakes his head, a shit-eating grin on his face as he watches Mom do as I say, then he turns his crazed eyes back on me. "Let's see if you actually have a set of balls on you because right now, I'm sure all I'll find is a pussy."

I clench my jaw while holding his gaze.

He lets out another bark of laughter. "See, all talk and no action. You're a fucking disgrace." He waves a fist in the air. "All of you are. I fucking bust my ass at the office for this family, and what thanks do I get?" He takes a threatening step closer to me. "Fucking disrespect. That's what."

In the past, I used to be scared shitless whenever he was like this, but after growing used to it, I hardly feel any emotion now.

The impassive expression I give Dad turns his face red with rage, and he lunges at me. Grabbing hold of my shirt, he shoves me against the wall while spitting, "Don't give me that look. You're nothing but human waste."

I bite my tongue, not giving him any reaction, and it only enrages him more.

"Colton." Hearing my name snaps me out of the past, and my eyes shoot up. Mr. Donati gives me a concerned look as he places a hand on my shoulder. He keeps his voice low as he asks, "Are you okay?"

"Yes, sir," I mutter, shifting uneasily in my chair.

He nods, giving my shoulder a squeeze before he continues with class.

Shit, it's the first time something like that happened. I've never had flashbacks before.

I clear my throat, and picking up a pen, I scribble on a page to keep my hand busy, but when I notice I'm trembling, I shove both my hands under the desk and clasp them tightly together. My heart is still beating like crazy as if it just happened.

That was the first time my father beat me so severely I couldn't go to school for two weeks. We used meningitis as an excuse.

The bell rings, and while I'm gathering my stuff, Mr. Donati walks to me and places a piece of paper on my desk. "That's my number. If you need to talk, just call. It doesn't matter what the time is."

Taking hold of the paper, I glance up at him.

None of my previous teachers cared. I was more off *sick* than at school toward the end of last year, and that's part of the reason I have to repeat my senior year.

I begin to say, "I'm fi –" but Mr. Donati shakes his head.

"You're not, Colton. I'd like to help but if you can't talk to me, then go meet with the counselor. You need to talk to someone about what happened."

I rise to my feet and shrug my bag's strap over my shoulder. Shoving the paper with his number into the inside pocket of my jacket, I mutter, "Talking won't change the

77

past." I walk to the door but then guilt creeps into my chest, and I pause. Glancing back at the teacher, I say, "Mr. Donati."

"Yes." His eyes lock on mine.

"Thanks for caring, though."

Mr. Donati's lips curve into a compassionate smile before I walk out of the classroom.

After the day from hell, I just want to go home, but I only make it to the lockers when I hear a loud bang, and my eyes dart toward the sound.

Michael has Brie pushed up against the lockers, and not thinking twice, I stalk toward them.

"No," Brie whimpers while trying to free herself from his hold.

"No?" he sneers. "I thought you needed the money."

I slide an arm between them and shove Michael away from Brie. Glancing at her, I snap, "Finish up so we can leave."

I turn my gaze back to Michael, who's glaring darkly at me. Then a smirk forms on his face. "Oh, brother, you're really begging for a beating."

"I'm not your brother." I take a step closer to him. "Leave her alone."

"Don't tell me you're into the weirdo," he chuckles.

I give him a look of warning before glancing back to Brie. I wait for her to shut the locker then take hold of her arm. She's so petite, it feels like I'll break her bones if I tighten my grip too hard.

The moment we're out of the building, she pulls her arm free from my hold.

"Seriously?" Michael laughs as he follows behind us. "I didn't take you for a freak lover. I actually thought you were badass. Such a fucking shame."

I know if I leave Brie here, the asshole will probably continue to bully her. I gesture to where my truck is parked. "I'll give you a ride home."

"Holy shit, will you look at that," Michael hollers. "Freak managed to get herself some dick."

I open the passenger door and snap, "Get in."

Brie hesitates, then shakes her head. "I'll walk."

Tilting my head, I lean down so I can catch her eyes and only manage to hold them for a moment before she focuses on our feet. "You're wasting my time. Get in so I can drop you off at home."

Again she hesitates, but then she gets in. I slam the door shut, and walking around the front of the car, I mumble, "This day is un-fucking-believable."

Michael walks up to me, and I notice a group of girls trailing behind him. He's just like Sully. An arrogant bastard who thinks he can do whatever he pleases.

"You're picking the wrong side," Michael warns.

"Baby, let's go," one of the girl's whines. "I want to get to Devil's Bluff before everyone else."

I climb behind the steering wheel and shove my bag into the space at Brie's feet. Starting the engine, I give Michael the same look I always gave my father – impassive as fuck.

I reverse out of the parking, and unable to contain my anger, I bark, "Why do you let them push you around?"

Brie doesn't answer me until I steer the vehicle down the road. She sounds scared shitless as she mumbles, "It's not like I have a choice."

I glance at her and take in how she's cowering against the door. "You have zero survival skills," I snap.

Her eyes dart to me just as I turn my gaze back to the road ahead.

"You can drop me off right here. I'll walk the rest of the way," she rambles.

I glance at her again, and seeing the uneasy look on her face, I force myself to calm down.

"We live on the same street. You can ride with me from now on."

"No… thanks."

"It wasn't a question," I state as I stop at a traffic light.

"But… you don't have to pick me up," she mutters.

I swear, a summer breeze could blow this girl right off the face of the planet. It's infuriating.

"They won't stop until you stand up for yourself." Brie doesn't respond to what I said, and it makes me grit my teeth. "It will only get worse."

Brie stares out of the window, her arms wrapped tightly over her chest.

God, give me strength!

"Brie!" I snap, and it has her eyes darting to me. "I won't always be there to stop Michael and Sully." I take a breath, then add, "Or your mother."

A look of helplessness makes the color of her eyes turn darker as she whispers, "I never asked you to."

I let out a frustrated sigh. There's no getting through to her.

Just like with Brady.

I turn up her driveway, and it has Brie gasping, "Right here is fine."

"I'll be here just after seven. Don't make me wait," I mention as she pushes the passenger door open.

She nods as she climbs out, then she hesitates and first glances up the road before asking, "Do you really live at number twenty-nine?"

"Yeah."

She begins to shut the door, then quickly says, "Have a good night."

I watch her walk up the driveway before I head home, wondering if I'll ever be able to make her understand that she has to fight back.

Chapter 6

BRIE

With my mother not home to keep time of how long I bathe, I fill the tub and even add some bubble bath that I stole from her bathroom.

I slip into the warm water, and when I lie back, a smile spreads over my face. I gather a bunch of bubbles in the palm of my hand and watch as they pop.

It's so nice having the house to myself, and I wish I could live on my own. Something small and far away from any town. Maybe a cottage in the mountains. Definitely, something cozy that's not near other people.

I could grow my own vegetables and fruits. I could have chickens.

I pull a face at the thought. I won't be able to hurt them, and I'd end up becoming a vegetarian or vegan.

A happy sigh escapes my lips as I close my eyes and sink deeper into the water.

I'd have a long bath every day. I'd have a room with lots of light where I can sketch. I'd hum a tune while preparing dinner. I'd binge-watch a show on TV surrounded by snacks.

I wouldn't be careful not to make a noise. I'd sleep all day and stay up all night.

I'd paint all the walls in different colors, and it will be like living in a rainbow. I'll get a puppy, and he'll love me.

I wouldn't have to ask permission for anything.

No one hurting me. No fear.

Just me living happily in my house.

———————————

I wake up and stretch out, a smile playing around my lips because I slept right through the night. I didn't even have any dreams.

The past couple of days have been pure bliss.

Mom's coming back today.

The thought makes a heaviness weigh down on me, and my shoulders slump as I climb out of bed.

Walking to the bathroom to brush my teeth and wash my face, I soak in the peacefulness around me one last time.

She'll probably be back when I get home from school.

After I'm done with my morning routine, and I'm dressed for school, I grab my bag then leave the house.

I'm hesitant about riding to school with Colton. It's already been a week, and he hasn't bullied me. He even stood up to Michael and Sully for me, and though he made me feel like I'm a nuisance, it doesn't take away from the fact that Colton helped me.

No one has ever tried to help me.

I stop by Colton's mailbox and stare at the house. The garden is pretty. The front door opens, and my heart beats a little faster as I watch Colton walk to the truck. His gait still gives off the impression that he's prowling for prey.

Should I ride with him or find a place to hide while I still can?

Dang, I'm running out of time. I need to decide now.

Maybe we can become friends?

He's a lot bigger than me, and the bullies will leave me alone then.

I'm still in two minds as the truck reverses down the driveway. Colton glances to his right, then to the left. His eyes skim over me and then instantly dart back, and the truck jerks to a sudden stop.

Not wanting to annoy him, I dart forward. Opening the door, I'm careful not to step on Colton's bag as I climb into the cab.

Sitting next to him, a familiar feeling of apprehension slithers down my spine as I mumble, "Morning."

Maybe this is a mistake.

"Morning." Colton checks the road, and as he reverses onto it, he says, "Put on your seatbelt."

I quickly do it and then stare at the street ahead.

"Did you sleep okay?" Colton suddenly asks.

I nod. "Yeah." There's a pause before I ask, "And you?"

"Yeah."

The atmosphere feels so awkward it makes my neck and face heat.

Colton must notice because he asks, "Are you okay?"

I nod and swallow hard before I explain, "I'm just awkward around people." I dare a glance in his direction and see the corner of his mouth lifting.

Is he going to laugh at me?

"Me too."

His words stun me, and I end up staring at him. "Really?"

"Yeah." A grin forms on his face, and he doesn't look as scary anymore. "People tend to suck."

Maybe we can be friends, or at least get along like Aspen and I do.

Feeling hopeful, the corners of my mouth lift, and I don't feel so uneasy anymore.

COLTON

I was surprised when I saw Brie waiting at my house. Yeah, I said she can ride with me, but I didn't think she would.

When we walk into school together, it feels like all eyes are on us. Brie falls back a couple of steps, and I wonder if she doesn't want to be seen with me.

Glancing over my shoulder at her, I joke, "Too late to worry about your image now."

"What?" she gasps and shaking her head, she catches up to me. "I was worried about your image."

I let out a chuckle. "I don't care what everyone thinks."

"Damn, you should," Sully says from behind us. He shoves Brie hard, making her stumble.

Turning around, I shove him back. "Don't touch her."

Sully lets out a burst of laughter and manages to not lose his balance. "So, it's true?" He shakes his head. "I thought everyone was talking shit, but you're really into her."

Brie scurries to her locker, and as I walk by her to get to mine, I snap, "You really need to start standing up for yourself."

If she doesn't start defending herself, they'll never stop, and it makes me so damn frustrated.

I grab my book for English as Brie darts down the hallway and disappears around the corner. A sigh escapes my lips, and I shake my head.

"So, are you really into Brie?" Sully asks as he leans a shoulder against the locker next to mine. "Because you're wasting your time with that one." A bunch of girls passes by us, and he points at one. "Get someone with an ass like that." He bites his bottom lip as he checks the girl out.

I slam the locker shut, and glaring at Sully, I growl, "Stay away from Brie."

"Or what?" he laughs.

I glare darkly at Sully until he becomes uncomfortable, and an uneasy smile forms on his face. He rams his shoulder against mine as he walks away.

I've lost count of how many times Brie was bullied today.

It's infuriating.

Once we're driving down the main road, I grumble, "Why do you let them push you around?"

When she doesn't answer, I glance at her. There's a frown on her forehead, and she's nibbling her bottom lip. She looks as frustrated as I feel.

Finally, she mumbles, "What am I supposed to do?"

"Fight back," I snap.

Her gaze darts to me, and for the first time, I see something close to anger flash over her face. But it's gone as quickly as it came.

"They're bigger than me," she states the obvious.

"Yeah, but they're only picking on you because you allow it," I argue. "Tell them to go to hell."

"It doesn't work," she mutters.

"Then report them."

She lets out an annoyed sigh. "I've tried that, and nothing gets done."

"So you're just going to take it?" I ask, exasperated.

She doesn't answer me, and I shake my head, not happy at all. I wish I knew how to get through to her.

"I'll walk from your house," she says, and it makes me wonder whether she doesn't want her mom to know that she rides with me. I don't ask, and the instant I bring the truck to a stop in my driveway, Brie scrambles out. "Have a good night."

My eyes go to the rearview mirror, and I watch until she's out of sight before I get out.

With a heavy feeling in my chest, I walk into the house. I'm frustrated and... scared. It looks like Brie's already given up, and it feels like I'm running out of time to help her.

Chapter 7

BRIE

The slap against the back of my head sends me stumbling forward, and I slam into the counter.

"You're just like her!" Mom shouts. I hunch my shoulders, keeping my body turned sideways.

Since my mother got home, she's been ranting about Kingsley Hunt living the life she should've had.

"It should've been me," she cries again. "Because of her, he ruined me instead of marrying me."

She's referring to Mason Chargill. When my mother tried to drown Kingsley, she got sentenced to probation for what she did, and Mason Chargill exposed my grandfather for fraud. My mother was shunned from the wealthy circle she belonged to and lost her social status. Mason and Kingsley got married, and from what I can tell, they're happy.

Unlike Mom.

"Just looking at you exhausts me to my core," She cries furiously. "You should've colored your hair like I told you to." My mother moves, and I flinch, but instead of hitting me again, she goes to open a drawer. When she pulls out a pair of scissors, fear prickles over my skin. I begin to shake my head, and the instant she takes a step toward me, I dart away and run for the safety of my room.

My heartbeat explodes into a frantic pounding.

"Get back here!" I feel her fingers claw at my back, and my body lurches forward. I take the stairs two at a time, and dashing into my room, I slam the door shut behind me.

There's a bang against it, and the doorknob wiggles. "Open this goddamn door!" Mom screams, shoving hard against it.

I grab hold of the knob and hold on tight while using all my strength to keep her from coming in.

Another thud has me crying, "Stop!" I suck in an anguished breath. "Please." She continues to hammer against the door, and I whimper, "Stop."

I struggle to keep her out and have to push my body against the door every time she manages to bump it open.

"If it's the last thing I do, I will cut your hair," she hysterically rages. "Open the door!"

Desperation and terror make me hold out until she stabs at the door with the scissors. The blades break through the wood, and it has me recoiling. I run to the windows on the other side of my bed, but before I can try to escape, the door slams open, and my mother storms into the room. A whack to the back of my head makes me crash against the windows. She hits me again, and grabbing hold of my shoulders, she shoves me to the floor.

I try to scramble free, but she crouches over me, pressing her knee into my stomach. All I can see is her venomous face and the scissors gleaming right above me.

Terror shudders through me, and it feels as if my blood is being chilled.

I try to grab hold of her arms, crying, "No, Mommy."

"Hold still!" When I keep struggling, the back of her hand strikes across my cheek. "I swear I'll stab you if you keep fighting me." The threat sends shockwaves through me.

She grabs a fistful of hair, and I hear the blades crunch close to my ear. "This is your fault. If you had gone to the hairdresser, I wouldn't have to cut this shit off myself."

Hopelessness, unlike anything I've felt before, fills every part of me. A broken cry tears out of me, and I bring my arms up to try and shield myself, but it only earns me more wild smacks from my mother. My arms burn and ache from the slaps, but I manage to cover my face with my hands.

Make it stop. Please!

With each snip, it feels as if the world closes in on me, suffocating me. There's a sharp pain above my ear when the scissors dig into my skin. As she continues to cut my hair, the blades nick and gash at my scalp.

It feels like endless hours of torture pass before Mom finally gets up, leaving me lying amongst heaps of hair. I drag myself into a sitting position and cover the cut above my ear with a trembling hand, feeling utterly distressed and terrified.

Mom walks to the door but then stops, and it makes me cringe into the corner between the bedside table and the wall. She glances at me, abhorrence making her look evil. Reaching a hand to the door, her pointer finger circles one of the holes she stabbed into it. "It's just wood and hair." Her gaze turns back to me, and then she lets out an irritated huff. "You're so goddamn dramatic. If I were going to kill you, I certainly wouldn't do it here. I'm not about to make a mess in my house."

She takes a step toward me again, and it makes my muscles tighten painfully. My body shakes violently with horror, and I cover my head with my arms.

She stops close to me, and I feel her breath waft over my arms, and then she whispers sinisterly, "No, I'd take you up to Devil's Bluff and shove you off one of the cliffs. I'll make it look like a suicide."

I hear her move away, and after a couple of minutes, I dare to peek from between my arms. Not seeing her, I cautiously climb to my feet. My eyes keep darting between the window and the entrance to my room, and taking a chance, I yank the window open. Climbing out, I don't care that I might hurt myself, and I jump to the lawn below. Landing, the impact sends pinpricks of pain up my feet and calves.

"Brie!" I hear my mother shout from somewhere inside, and icy terror has me breaking out into a run. I sprint across the lawn and down the driveway. Not caring where I'm going, my bare feet slap against the pavement as I dart up the street.

The ordeal shudders through me, and sobs break free from the tightness in my chest, making it hard to gasp for air.

I can't handle this anymore.

I want to die.

I wish she would die.

What's the point of life if hatred is all I'll ever know. Other kids have parents who love them. They get smiles and hugs where all I get is rage and pain.

Life is just... hell.

COLTON

"I just need time," Mom says.

My eyes are glued to her, where she's on a call with Dad. Apprehension tightens my stomach into a tense knot.

"I know, Jonah. I'll think about it." She listens to whatever he says then mumbles, "You too. Bye."

"What did he want?" I ask, unable to keep the worry from making my tone harsh.

"He wants us to move back to California."

My heart sinks heavily as dread tightens my insides. "No." The word explodes from me. "There's no way! Don't tell me you're actually thinking about it."

"I don't know what to do," she whimpers, and her face crumbles, anxiety making her dark brown eyes look bruised.

"Tell him no, Mom," I snap. "Just say no."

"It's not that easy," she cries.

Frustration begins to suffocate me, and I walk out of her room before I do or say something I'll regret. I keep going, right out of the house and down the driveway.

Someone crashes into me, and we both hit the pavement hard. For a split second, Brie's terrified face hovers over me, and then she's up and running away.

I shoot to my feet and manage to catch up to her. Grabbing hold of her arm, I pull her to a stop a couple of houses from mine.

"Nooo!" Brie cries desperately, but I tighten my hold on her arm so she can't pull free.

"Wait," I say hurriedly. "Just wait a second."

"Let go. Let go. Let go," she chants frantically, trying to twist her arm free, and it's only then I see the blood on her neck.

What the hell?

Knowing I need to calm Brie down, I pull her to me and wrap my arms around her. "Shhh." She keeps struggling

97

against my hold, but I tighten my grip so she won't yank free. "I'm not going to hurt you. Let me help."

My words must get through to her because the fight drains out of her. Her whole frame shudders as she cries against my chest.

"Can we go to my house?" I ask. "It's better there than out here on the street."

I pull a little back, trying to see her face, but she covers it with trembling hands.

My God. What happened to her?

I can't see much outside in the dark and keeping my tone soft, so I don't scare her, I say, "Let's go inside."

Her movements are fitful as she nods.

I keep an arm around her quivering shoulders, and walking back to my house, Brie folds her arms tightly around her waist.

When I manage to get Brie inside, I let out a sigh of relief. I steer her down the hallway to the bathroom then softly say, "Sit on the toilet."

Brie keeps standing, her whole body tense as if she'll run at any given moment.

"You're safe here. No one will hurt you," I try to offer her some sense of security.

My eyes drift over Brie and what I see makes a familiar horror chill me to my bones. I move forward, and framing her face, I take in the blood and jagged strands, gasping, "God, did your mom do this?"

Brie tries to pull away, but I lean down and lock eyes with her. There's so much torment in her blue irises, it's hard to look into them. "I have to see if any of the cuts need stitches." There's also blood on her right cheek, arms, and hands.

Breaths shudder over her lips, and her skin is deathly pale. She tries to swallow a sob down, making a pitiful sound that has my heart shrinking.

Moving my attention to her head, my stomach rolls when I see half of her hair has been cut haphazardly, and there are lots of cuts. I inspect them, but I can't see properly with the blood. I reach for the facecloth and rinse it under the water until it's lukewarm.

"I'm sorry if it hurts," I murmur before I begin to wipe the worst of the blood away.

Brie lifts a trembling hand to the right side of her head and points above her bloody ear. "This side hurts most." She sounds petrified, her voice hoarse and quivering from the trauma she must've suffered.

I should be used to seeing this kind of violence, but it still rocks me to my core.

I step closer and move the jagged strands of hair out of the way. After carefully cleaning the cut, I reassure her, "It doesn't look like you need stitches."

All the beatings my father gave me have made me an expert when it comes to taking care of wounds.

I pause for a moment to breathe because it's so damn hard to look at what's been done to her.

It's sadistic and gut-wrenching.

The same thing has been done to me.

Memories of the abuse I suffered at the hands of my father for so many years flash through me. Bile pushes up my throat, but I swallow it down.

Brie needs you.

The thoughts help to steel me against the onslaught of empathy I feel for Brie. There's an overwhelming connection to her, knowing how she must feel right now.

I continue to clean the cuts, then move down to her cheek and neck. When I wipe the blood from her arms and hands, I'm relieved when I don't find more wounds.

For the first time in my life, I allow myself to remember what I felt right after a beating, so I'll know how to handle Brie.

Once I've done the best I can, I tilt my head and lean down so I can catch her eyes, but she quickly lowers her gaze to the floor. Slowly, I lift my hand, and placing a finger beneath her chin, I gently nudge her face up until her eyes dart to mine.

"You're safe here," I assure her again. She probably doesn't believe me, and I know I'll have to repeat it a lot before it will sink in.

Her gaze flits away from mine, and her tongue darts out to wet her lips.

"Are you thirsty? I can make coffee or tea. Whatever you prefer."

Brie shakes her head but then croaks, "Water." She swallows hard and quickly adds, "Please."

When I walk out of the bathroom, Brie darts forward and sticks close to me. An overpowering urge to hold her fills my chest, and I clench my hands into fists, so I don't reach for her because I seriously doubt she wants to be touched right now.

I take a glass out of the cupboard and fill it with cold water from the fridge. When Brie takes it from me, I notice that she's still trembling.

My gaze flits over her, and again I take in how badly she's been hurt. There are swollen red marks on both her arms.

My arms looked like that from trying to block the punches from my father.

The horrifying sight delivers a blow to my gut, almost knocking me off balance.

I wait until she takes a couple of sips before I say, "You're going to be okay." I want her to know it will get better.

I'll make sure of it.

Brie chokes on the water, and before I can reach for the glass, it drops from her hands and shatters at our feet.

She covers her mouth with both her hands, and through the fit of coughs, her eyes fly to my face. There's so much terror in her gaze, and she begins to back away from me as if I'll hurt her.

"It's nothing," the words rush from me. "It's okay. Don't panic." She stills for a moment but then moves her hands up to cover her face as her shoulders begin to jerk.

I can't just stand and watch, and stepping over the mess, I reach for Brie and pull her against my chest. I lower my head and begin to whisper, "I know how you feel. I know it hurts."

She moves her hands away from her face and turns her head, resting her cheek against me as a sob escapes her.

She needs to know she's not alone.

"I've been through the same thing. You can trust me."

Chapter 8

BRIE

My nerves feel stretched thin, and anguish keeps hitting me in waves. My emotions keep fluctuating between calming down and panicking.

The moment Colton wraps his arms around me, the dam wall breaks, and I lose control over the tears. I'm flooded with something I haven't felt before – warmth and safety. It makes me feel like I'm a human being and not… nothing.

Goosebumps spread over my skin, and I begin to cry for a different reason – because someone is showing me kindness.

Colton tightens his arms around me, and I hear him whisper, "You're not alone anymore."

Overwhelmed, sobs wrack me. It feels like I've been starved to death, and in desperate need to feel safe, I wrap my arms around Colton's waist and bury my face between his chest and my bicep.

I'm violently tossed from one emotion to the next. From experiencing a hug for the first time, and the comfort it gives, to absolute heartbreak because I've never had this before.

"What happened?" I hear a woman ask, and I'm ripped back to the cold terror that's my constant reality.

I yank away, and my eyes wildly search for an exit.

"Don't come closer, Mom," Colton calls out, holding a hand up toward her.

He reaches for me with his other hand, and I quickly move to his side.

When he wraps an arm around my shoulders, he says, "It's okay. My mom won't hurt you."

I glance back at Colton's mom, and when she smiles, it does nothing to lessen the anxiety I feel.

Please don't let them hurt me. Please.

There's a concerned look on Mrs. Lawson's face as she stares at me, and it sets me a little at ease.

"Shouldn't we take her to the hospital?" She asks.

NoNoNo.

I shake my head and glancing up at Colton, I whisper, "I can't go there. It will make my mother angrier."

"She doesn't need stitches," he tells his mom.

"But she could have internal injuries," Mrs. Lawson argues.

"I don't!" And then I repeat the words my mother has said hundreds of times to me, "It's not so bad."

Get over it. Stop being so dramatic.

"My God," Mrs. Lawson gasps. "Your hair."

Humiliation spreads through me like a raging fire, and feeling dreadfully self-conscious, I lift my hand to what's left of my hair.

"You can fix it, right?" Colton asks his mom.

My eyes dart back to her, and there's a weird sensation in my chest as an empathetic smile pulls at her mouth.

"Yes." She takes a cautious step closer, and I instantly tense next to Colton. "I can cut it into a pixie style if you want?"

Cut.

I shake my head, and when I try to take a step backward, I'm stopped by Colton's arm that's still around my shoulders. My chin begins to tremble as apprehension fills my chest, snuffing out the little calmness I've managed to gain.

"We don't have to do anything now," Colton reassures me. "It can wait."

Unable to cope with everything that's happened, it's becoming increasingly hard to not cry.

Then Colton asks, "Have you had dinner? I was just about to prepare something."

"Dinner?" I ask, and it makes me aware of the hollowness in my stomach. "You want me to stay for dinner?"

It's such a foreign concept that I can't wrap my mind around it.

"You can't go home," Colton says. He glances at his mom before he continues, "You can stay here as long as you like."

Home. My mother.

She'll be so mad because I left.

Fear drives me to ask, "If it's okay, can I stay the night?" Not wanting to get in trouble, I quickly add, "I won't get in the way."

I just need tonight to gather my strength before I have to face my mother again.

Mrs. Lawson gives me a gentle smile. "Colton is right. You can stay as long as you want." She gestures to me. "I can give you some of my clothes to change into."

"You can go bathe or shower if you want," Colton adds. "I'll start dinner."

I glance down at the bloodstains on my t-shirt.

Clean clothes would be nice.

Mrs. Lawson smiles at me again.

I want to believe that she's nice, but life has taught me people are cruel.

When I keep still, Colton moves his hand to my back. "Mom, will you mind picking something and bringing it here?"

"Sure." I watch until she disappears down the hallway.

Colton moves in front of me, and my gaze darts up to his face. I take in the nose ring and his dark eyes. All this time, I thought he'd become a bully, but I was wrong.

So wrong.

He's done nothing but be kind to me. The longer I look at him, the more it feels like he sees right into the heart of me.

I so badly want a hug again, it makes my vision blur with tears as I whisper, "Thank you."

Seconds tick by, and then the corner of Colton's mouth lifts. It's like sunshine breaking through stormy clouds. He steps closer, and when his arms wrap around me, I feel the warmth of a thousand suns shine down on me.

And for a breathless moment, I don't feel utterly alone.

———————————

COLTON

I hold Brie until I hear Mom walk back into the kitchen. The last time I felt so protective of anyone was Brady, and the feeling comes naturally as if I've known Brie all my life.

It's because we share the same story.

I pull back and take hold of Brie's hand. "Let's get you cleaned up." Brie follows behind me, and I stop to take the clothes from Mom. "Thanks. I'll start dinner in a couple of minutes."

"It's okay. I'll throw something together while you take care of..."

She gives me a questioning look, and I quickly answer, "Brie. She's the girl I told you about. The one who draws."

"Oh." A wide smile spreads over Mom's face.

Only when I walk toward the bathroom does it hit me like a ton of bricks that Mom's out of her bedroom, and she's going to prepare dinner.

Shock ripples over me, and then a smile forms around my lips as a thought creeps into my mind.

We can help Brie, and just maybe... Brie can help Mom.

God, I hope so.

I set the clothes down on the counter and turn to Brie, and instead of seeing a broken girl, I see hope.

Still smiling like an idiot, I say, "You can bathe or shower." I glance around, then add, "Everything you'll need should be here."

My gaze falls on the towels. I haven't changed them yet this week.

"Give me a second." I dart out into the hallway and going to the linen closet, I grab fresh towels.

When I walk back into the bathroom, Brie hasn't moved a muscle. I set the towels down next to the clothes and grab the dirty ones. "Just shout if you need anything."

I walk to the door, and when I begin to pull it shut, Brie says, "I'll be quick."

I pause and smile at her. "No rush. Take your time."

I'm sure she needs some alone time to process everything.

I walk back to the kitchen, and when I see Mom's boiling water, another wave of relief washes over me.

"Is it really okay with you if she stays with us?" I ask while walking over to where Mom is.

"Of course. That's not even a question. She can't go back home," Mom gasps. She puts spaghetti in the water and turns to me. "She can't go to school either."

"I know." I draw my bottom lip between my teeth. "Will you be okay with her here during the day. I don't want to fall behind with classes."

Mom places her hand on my arm. "It will be nice to have someone here."

Just then, Brie peeks around the corner of the hallway, and I walk closer, asking, "Do you need something?"

She shakes her head and steps forward. It hasn't even been five minutes, but she's dressed in clean clothes. The sweatpants are a bit long, so Brie rolled them up.

"Are you done already?" I ask.

Brie nods, and her eyes dart to where Mom is.

Shit. I should've realized it earlier.

Where I'm cautious around men because my father was the abuser, Brie's scared of women because her mother's been hurting her. She first has to get used to being around my mother if I'm going to leave the two of them alone tomorrow.

I gesture to the stool at the kitchen table. "Do you want to sit down?"

Brie gives me an unsure look, so I take her hand and pull her into the kitchen. I sit down first, then nudge the stool next to me closer to her. Brie keeps glancing at Mom as she cautiously takes a seat.

"The food will take a couple of minutes," Mom says. Walking over to the fridge, she opens it, asking, "Can I pour you something to drink, Brie? We have lemonade, orange juice, and coke."

Brie stares at Mom as if she just grew a pair of horns.

I place a hand on her back and lean forward. "What do you like to drink?"

She looks like a deer caught in headlights, but then she stammers, "C-coke." She swallows hard, then adds, "Please."

"I'll have some as well," I say. "Thanks, Mom."

Mom pours two glasses then places them in front of us. There's a confused expression on Brie's face.

Just from how she reacts to everything, it's obvious Brie's had it much worse than me.

I stare at the girl next to me, realizing she's not as weak as I thought.

"Is it just you and your mom?" I ask, wanting to know more about her life so I can help her better.

Brie nods. She hesitates for a moment but then reaches for the glass. This time I wait until she sets it down before I ask, "Has it always been like this?"

Her eyes dart to mine, and I watch the emotions ripple over her face. Fear, despair, and then the look she always has. I thought it was anxiety, but I now know it's from years of neglect.

Has this girl ever known any kind of love?

When Brie nods, I get all my answers, and it cracks my heart wide open. Not able to hold back, I get up and hug her again while empathy and anger mix in my chest.

How can someone do this to another human?

You know how. You've had a monster for a father.

But damn, at least I was loved by Mom and Brady, and I have never been bullied at school.

Brie has nowhere she feels safe.

Pulling away, I sit back down and ask, "Has no one tried to help?" Anger for everything she's been put through starts to burn through my veins.

"I called the police once," Brie answers, much to my surprise.

"What happened?" Mom asks, and it's only then I notice she's sitting on the other side of the table listening to our conversation.

113

"My mom told them I fell off a bike and was looking for attention."

When Brie doesn't continue, I ask, "And?"

Brie shrugs. "They scolded me and said if I ever made a call like that again, they'd arrest me."

"Mother of God," Mom gasps. "How old were you?"

Brie thinks for a moment, and a frown forms on her forehead. "Six or seven."

Holy shit.

Both Mom and I can only stare until Brie shifts uncomfortably in her chair.

"And school? Did no one ever notice anything?" I ask, even though I know most teachers look the other way or believe the lie you tell them.

"They just think I'm clumsy," Brie whispers.

I glance at Mom and see the tears shining in her eyes, and I know she remembers all the lies we told to keep our filthy secret. Mom catches me looking at her, and she quickly gets up to continue with the food.

I turn my attention back to Brie, and placing a hand on her shoulder, I say, "You have us now."

The saddest expression I've ever seen settles on her face as she slowly lifts her eyes to mine.

She's too scared to even hope.

I lean forward and move my hand to the back of her neck. My voice is filled with determination as I promise, "You have me now, Brie. I'll fight with you."

Chapter 9

BRIE

Mrs. Lawson places a pillow and blanket down on the couch, then turns to where I'm standing, and says, "Are you sure the couch is okay? There is a guest bedroom you can use."

I nod, wanting to be close to the front door. It makes me feel safer.

She glances at Colton, then smiles. "Call me if you need anything. Good night."

"Night," I mumble, my eyes following her until she disappears up the stairs.

"I'll be right back," Colton says.

I glance over my shoulder at the kitchen. There are dishes piled in the sink, and it makes my chest fill with apprehension. Mrs. Lawson said to leave it after cleaning up the mess I made when I dropped the glass.

My mother would kill me if the kitchen looked so untidy.

Colton comes back down the stairs carrying a pillow and blanket, and a frown begins to form on my forehead.

He sets it down on the other couch, then looks at me. "Want to watch some TV before we sleep?"

My lips part with surprise, and unconsciously wringing my hands, I ask, "Are you going to sleep down here, as well?"

"Yeah." He pauses for a moment, then asks, "Are you okay with it?"

It's not like I have a choice, so I nod.

"Are you going to sit down?"

"Y-yeah." I swallow hard on the anxious knot in my throat and inching closer to the couch, I gingerly sit down on the edge of the cushion.

I know Colton said I'm safe here and that he's going to help me, but... it's hard to trust.

Colton lies down on the other couch, and taking the remote from the coffee table, he switches on the TV. "What do you want to watch?"

When I take too long to answer, he turns his head to me. My eyes dart between his and the TV before I admit, "I don't usually watch TV."

His eyebrows lift. "We can sleep if you don't want to watch anything."

"No," the word burst from me. "I want to. It's just…" I feel super self-conscious when I continue, "I'm not allowed to watch TV at home. You can put anything on."

Colton signs into Netflix, and my eyes flit over all the shows I always hear the other students talk about at school.

He keeps scrolling then asks, "How do you feel about a documentary on the cutest animals? I think it will be relaxing."

"Okay."

The show starts, and my eyes are glued to the TV screen for a long while before they drift to where Colton lies on the other couch. He looks relaxed, and it makes me scoot back into a more comfortable position.

By the time an hour has passed, I feel it's safe enough to lie down on my side. For a couple of minutes, my eyes dart between Colton and the TV, and when he doesn't move or even glance my way, I relax into the cushion beneath me.

Everything at Colton's house is in total contrast with my own home. No one yells, and I haven't been snapped at once.

They're so nice.

The last animal I remember seeing is a baby goat, and then I drift off to sleep.

COLTON

When credits begin to roll over the screen, I dare a glance in Brie's direction.

Seeing she's asleep, a smile spreads over my face. I switch off the TV and decide to leave the kitchen light on for Brie. Turning onto my side, my eyes stay glued to her.

All the frustration I felt earlier because Brie wouldn't stand up for herself is gone. In its place is an overwhelming need to keep her safe.

My thoughts turn to my mother and how different she was tonight. It's as if Brie drew her out of the depression.

I know Mom said it's okay for Brie to stay here, but I'll have to talk to her about it because there's no way Brie can go back to her mother.

I'll go with Brie to get her stuff so her mother can't do anything. She can move into the guest room.

I begin to drift off when Brie begins to move restlessly, and I hear her desperately mumble, "No… Stop."

I'm up in an instant, and darting to the other couch, I sit down next to her. I place my hand on her shoulder. "Brie, wake up."

She's trembling like a leaf in a shit storm, gasping, "Sto-op."

I shake her. "Brie."

Her eyes fly open, and she darts up, her chest slamming into mine. I quickly move an arm around her. Her breaths explode in my ear, and then she wraps her arms around my neck. The way she holds onto me makes a foreign sensation spread through me.

"Are you okay?" I whisper.

She nods, and I feel her ear brush against mine.

I want to comfort her so desperately, it has me asking, "Want me to lie with you for a little bit?"

She hesitates for a moment but then scoots over to make space for me. Keeping my arm around her shoulders, I pull her tightly into my side as I lie down. I bring my other hand to her cheek and lowering my head, I press a soft kiss to the top of her head. "Things will get better."

Brie curls up against me, resting her cheek on my chest.

Wanting to distract her, I ask, "What's your favorite color?"

"All of them," she whispers. "Yours?"

"Blue." I hope she won't take it the wrong way as I add, "Like your eyes. They remind me of the ocean." A couple of seconds pass, then I ask, "Have you thought about what you want to do once we graduate?"

"I'd like to attend art school."

"Yeah?" My thumb lightly brushes over her jaw, and I take in how soft her skin is. "You're really good at drawing."

There's a moment's silence, then Brie asks, "And you?"

"I'm going to work."

I feel the tension begin to ease out of her as she whispers, "What kind of work?"

"Anything," I answer. "I'm not picky."

"Don't you want to study further?" I take it as a good sign that she's asking questions.

"Nah, I want to be able to look after my mother."

And you, if you come to live with us.

"Why do you have so many piercings?"

The question catches me by surprise, and the corner of my mouth lifts. "It keeps people at a distance."

"I should get a bunch too," she mumbles.

A comfortable silence falls around us, and I begin to grow sleepy again when Brie murmurs, "Why are you so nice to me?"

I knew she'd ask that at some point. "I've been through something similar."

Brie moves a little back, and her eyes drift over my face. "But how? You're strong and never let Michael or Sully bully you."

I keep my eyes locked on hers as I admit, "My father was stronger."

Brie stares at me, then she asks, "Where is he now?"

"In California. We left after –" The words cut off, and sucking in a deep breath of air against the grief, I glance around the living room. "Brady, my brother, committed suicide because he couldn't take it anymore."

Brie nods, too much understanding on her face, and instead of it offering me any comfort, it makes my insides knot up with worry.

"Suicide is never the answer," I say, my voice sounding harsher than I mean for it to be. "There's always something to live for."

"Like?" The word is so soft I almost think it was my imagination.

"Brady had me. He had my mother and a girlfriend. We all loved him, and I did my best to take the brunt of our father's rages. He had a lot to live for."

Brie rests her head on my shoulder again, and after a while, she whispers, "What if you don't have anyone?"

I know she's referring to herself. "But you do." I tighten my arm around her shoulders and press another kiss to the top of her head. "You have me."

Her voice quivers with emotion as she asks, "Are we friends now?"

The answer comes easily. "Definitely."

Brie stirs slightly, and I notice her hand is fisted as it lies in the middle of my chest. I move mine from her cheek and slowly begin to pry her fingers open until I can press her palm flat over my shirt.

Still worried about leaving her alone with Mom, I ask, "Will you be okay to stay with my mom tomorrow while I go to school?"

Apprehension tightens her voice, "I have to go home."

"You don't," I argue. "You can stay with us."

Brie shakes her head. "It won't be right, and my mom will get angry."

I shift my hand to her chin and nudge her face up. When our eyes meet, I say, "She can't hurt you if you're here."

With the light shining in from the kitchen, I see the concern on Brie's face.

She doesn't trust me yet.

"We can take it a day at a time. Get to know us, and once you trust us, you can decide if you want to move in," I offer an alternative that won't be as daunting as immediately moving in.

I can see she's thinking about what I just said, and then she nods. "Okay."

Worried for her safety, I say, "Can you wait until after school tomorrow so I can go with you to your house. Maybe if your mom sees you have someone who cares, she'll be careful."

Brie stares at me as if I just said the unthinkable, and then the corner of her mouth lifts slightly. "You care?" Her eyes begin to shine, and she sucks in a shaky breath. "About me?"

"Yeah." My answer makes a tear spiral over her cheek, and using my thumb, I wipe it away. "Can I ask you a question?"

She sniffs then nods.

"Has anyone ever cared about you?"

A neglected expression shadows her face, and I can see she's struggling not to cry, then she whispers, "No." She swallows hard on the emotion, then admits, "You're the first person to hug me."

124

My God, it's so much worse than I thought.

The saddest emotions well in my chest, and turning my body toward her, I wrap both my arms tightly around her. I hug her as hard as I can without hurting her.

I feel a tremble ripple through her body and wish I could tuck her inside my heart where no one would be able to hurt her again.

Chapter 10

BRIE

Waking up, my head instantly clears of sleep when I feel Colton's chest rise and fall beneath my cheek and hand.

Memories of last night rush through me. It was both the worst and best night of my life, and the combination leaves me feeling over-emotional.

The ordeal with my mom was nothing short of horrifying, but... afterward, being with Colton... was wonderful. It still is.

Colton said he cares about me.

The memory makes a weird sensation flood my chest. It's something akin to finally finding a place where I belong. Not being alone anymore. It's an overwhelming feeling.

He's been so nice to me, and now that I've had a taste of safety, I really don't want to go back home. Or to school. I want to stay right here.

I start to smell something delicious, and pushing myself up, I peek over the couch. Seeing Mrs. Lawson in the

126

kitchen, my eyes widen, and I pat Colton frantically on his chest.

He lets out a groan, and when his eyes open, I whisper anxiously, "Your mom's in the kitchen."

Embarrassed that she must've seen us lying together burns through me. I scramble over Colton only to drop to the floor. Pushing up on my hands and knees, my wide eyes land on Colton's grinning face.

"It's okay," he chuckles, still half asleep.

I sit back in a kneeling position, not able to stop staring at Colton because he looks different first thing in the morning. There's a shadow forming on his jaw. My eyes drift over his face, and I realize he no longer looks dangerous, but instead...

Oh crap.

My hand flies to my heart that's starting to thump faster against my ribs, and I nervously wet my lips.

Climbing to my feet, my gaze darts over the living room, looking everywhere but at Colton.

"Oh good, you're up," Mrs. Lawson says from the kitchen. "I made a fresh pot of coffee."

It feels like my face is going up in flames as I mumble, "I need the restroom." I only realize what I just said once the words are out, which makes me blush even more.

127

Really, Brie? You didn't have to tell them you're going to pee.

I rush down the hallway.

Ugh, kill me now.

Once I shut the bathroom door behind me, I lean my forehead against it and suck in deep breaths to calm down.

What was that?

I've always felt awkward around people, but that was different.

I rub a hand over my excited heartbeat and draw my bottom lip between my teeth.

You're just thankful. That's probably all it is.

Pushing away from the door, my eyes catch my reflection as I pass the mirror. I stop dead in my tracks, and my eyes grow huge as I take in how awful I look.

My stomach drops to my feet, and as my eyes flit over the haphazard strands of what's left of my hair, my heart grows heavy.

I look ugly.

I was too upset last night to care about my appearance, but now that I've calmed down… I look horrid.

A lump pushes up my throat when I think of how everyone at school will tease me. Sadness spills into my chest until it forces tears to spiral down my cheeks.

I loved my hair. It was my protection against the world, and now… it's gone.

There's a knock at the door, then Colton calls, "Are you okay, Brie?"

I shake my head, and when I open my mouth to tell him I'll be out in a minute, a sob escapes instead.

"I'm coming in," I hear Colton say, and when the door starts to open, I quickly turn my back to it.

Now that I know what I look like, shame burns through me, and I don't want Colton seeing me like this.

I feel his hand on my lower back, and when he moves in next to me, I turn my face away from him. I wrap my arms around myself and hunch my shoulders, wishing I could just disappear.

"Hey," Colton whispers, and as if he knows exactly what I'm thinking, he says, "Your hair will grow back. Once my mom cuts it, it won't look so bad anymore."

The thought of having a pair of scissors near me fills me with apprehension, but I know I'll have to let Mrs. Lawson cut my hair, or I won't be able to go back to school.

Not wanting to be alone with her, I ask, "Can she do it now? I don't want to miss any classes and…" My words trail away because I don't want to offend Colton by saying I don't want to be here alone with his mom.

"Sure." His hand disappears from my back, and then I feel his fingers wrap around my hand, and he squeezes it. "Finish up in here, then come to the kitchen."

When his hand lets go of mine, I instantly miss the strength I felt.

Once the door shuts behind Colton, I quickly relieve myself, then wash my hands. I borrow some of the toothpaste, and using the tip of my finger, I brush my teeth.

When I'm done, I suck in a fortifying breath before I leave the bathroom.

I first peek around the corner, and seeing Colton and Mrs. Lawson standing by the stove, I slowly walk closer. I keep the kitchen table between us.

Not wanting to get in trouble for just standing around, I ask, "Can I help with anything?"

Mrs. Lawson turns to me and smiles. "No, dear. Why don't you get some coffee? Breakfast is almost ready."

Colton grabs two mugs out of a cupboard and pours coffee into them. "How do you drink yours?"

"Some sugar and cream, please." I move closer to him and nervously smile as I take a mug once he's done stirring the caramel liquid. "Thank you."

"We'll eat, and then my mom will help you with your hair," Colton says before taking a sip.

"Okay." I nurse the warm liquid while I watch Mrs. Lawson make eggs. She looks like a mom should – tender smiles and warmth radiating off her.

Once I'm done with my coffee, I clear my throat and say, "Thank you for letting me stay the night."

Mrs. Lawson glances at me, no aggression anywhere on her features. Her dark brown hair reaches just above her shoulders, and it doesn't look like she's brushed it.

Mom will never leave her bedroom without every hair in place and her make-up done.

Mrs. Lawson's wearing a robe over her pajamas.

Another thing Mom will never leave her room wearing.

Colton takes three plates from a cupboard and begins to set the table. Wanting to do something, I grab his mug from where he left it on the counter and walk to the sink.

Glancing over my shoulder at Mrs. Lawson, I ask, "Is it okay if I wash the dishes?"

"You don't have to, dear." She looks up from where her eyes were trained on the eggs. "I'll do them after the two of you head to school. It will give me something to do."

Oh wow, my mom will never wash dishes.

The differences between my mom and Mrs. Lawson are glaringly obvious, and it makes me feel less anxious around her.

When the food is ready, we sit down at the table, and just like the night before during dinner, there's no tension as we eat.

A feeling ripples through me, and it sends my heart racing. It almost feels ravenous.

I want more of this.

I want to be a part of a family that loves each other.

———————

COLTON

Brie is much more relaxed than last night, and it eases the worry that's been gnawing at my insides.

Once we're all done eating, Mom says, "Colton, will you place one of the chairs in the bathroom?"

"Sure." While I'm busy setting up everything for the haircut, Brie clears the table.

When we're done, I walk over to Brie, and I take hold of her elbow. Worried about the cuts on her head, I lean down and whisper, "How do the gashes feel?"

She lifts a hand to her head and pats over it. "Better."

"Let's make your hair beautiful again. Don't want you to be late for school," Mom says.

Brie hesitates before she answers, "Okay."

"Want me to come with?" I ask.

Brie nods and knowing she wants me there makes the same weird sensation from the night before ripple through my chest. I attribute it to just feeling protective of her.

I go sit on the closed toilet lid, so I'm out of the way.

"Can you wet your hair?" Mom asks while she reaches for a towel.

Brie wets it in the sink, and then Mom presses most of the water out before draping the towel around Brie's shoulders.

"Take a seat." Mom reaches for the scissors on the counter, and I watch as Brie's eyes widen when she notices.

I lean forward and place my hand over Brie's. "I'm here."

She turns her hand over, and grips tightly hold of mine.

Her eyes lock on my face, and when I see the fear in them, I say, "Wait a second, Mom." I reach forward and pull the chair with Brie closer until her knees are between mine.

"Just keep looking at me," I say to her.

Brie nods, and the moment I reach for her hand, her fingers wrap tightly around my palm.

I nod for Mom to proceed.

My eyes stay locked with Brie's as Mom begins to cut the remaining long strands. With every snip, Brie flinches. Tension hangs thick in the air, and I force a smile to my face, hoping it will make Brie feel better.

By the time Mom sets the scissors down, my stomach feels like a hard knot of nerves.

Letting out a tense breath, I ask, "Are you done?"

"Yes." Mom moves the towel from around Brie's shoulders and drops it in the basin. "Now, for the fun part. Let's go to my room so I can blowdry it."

When we get up, my eyes go over the new hairstyle, and seeing how good it looks, pride swells in my chest for the incredible job my mom did. "It looks good."

"Really?" Brie asks.

She turns to look at the mirror, but I stop her. "Let's finish first. I want you to see it once my mom's dried it."

Walking into Mom's room, I go sit on the unmade bed and watch as Mom styles Brie's hair. When Mom's done, she pulls at a couple of strands with her fingers, saying, "You can look."

Brie's eyes lift to the mirror in front of her, and then her lips part. A smile begins to waver around her lips before it stretches into a full-blown happy grin. "Gosh, thank you so much."

Mom cut it short like mine at the back, and at the front, the bangs are longer.

I stare at Brie's face, and then the realization hits – she's actually pretty with the long hair not hanging in her face. You can now see her eyes clearly.

Damn, she's really pretty.

There's a tightening feeling in my chest, and I swallow hard.

Holy shit, Brie's beautiful.

My eyes meet hers in the mirror's reflection, and then she asks, "Do you like it?"

"A lot," I admit before I'm able to deal with the new emotions. "You look good."

Her cheeks flush, and she quickly gets up. Turning to my mom, there's a grateful smile on Brie's face. "Thank you."

"Maybe we can play around with some make-up next time," Mom offers.

"O-okay."

Brie's obviously still cautious with my mother, but at least she doesn't look downright terrified anymore. It makes me smile, but then it fades when I remember we still have to go by her house for her uniform.

"I'm just going to get dressed. I'll be back in a couple of minutes."

I dart out of the room and rush through my morning routine. It's the quickest I've ever taken to get ready for school.

"I'll wash the clothes before I return them," I hear Brie say as I come down the stairs.

"Don't worry about it," Mom replies.

I find them standing by the front door and stop to press a kiss to Mom's cheek. "I'll see you later."

"Have a good day," she calls after us.

Chapter 11

BRIE

During the short ride to my house, all the good feelings I experienced at Colton's home fade, and in their place, familiar apprehension sets in.

I stop by the front door and suck in a deep breath. Before I reach for the knob, Colton's fingers wrap around mine.

"If anything happens, let me handle it," he says.

I turn my head and glance up at him. I remember the first time I saw him. I thought he would only be trouble.

Boy, was I wrong.

Colton walked right into my hell and started fighting for me, even though I never expected him to.

The front door suddenly swings open, and my mother glares at me. "Where the hell have you been?" Her eyes slant to Colton, and the sneer on her face deepens. "Seriously? You ran to him? I told you not to see him!"

My face warms with embarrassment because my mother's so rude to Colton.

She lifts a hand to reach for my arm, but Colton steps between us, and his voice is a deep rumble of warning as he says, "We're just here for her school uniform." Colton pushes my mother to the side, and he pulls me inside.

"What the hell?" Mom snaps.

Colton lets go of my hand and points to the stairs. "Go get dressed, Brie." Then he turns to face my mother and growls, "Back off. Your days of abusing Brie are over."

My mouth drops open with surprise when she doesn't lay into him, and I hurry to my room.

Wow, my mother's actually cautious with Colton here.

I've never seen her like that, and it makes her look less like a threat.

I change into my school clothes as quickly as I can, and grabbing my phone and bag, I rush back to where Colton is still glaring at my mother.

Not knowing what else to say, I stammer, "B-bye." And then I dart out of the door with Colton right behind me.

"I'll see you later," Mom says derisively, and her words promise nothing good for me.

Walking back to Colton's truck, I keep glancing up at his face that looks like a dark thunder cloud. I've seen so many sides to Colton in the past twenty-four hours, and knowing he's only been kind to me, I don't feel scared like I would've in the past.

"Thank you," I murmur. "For everything."

The dark expression fades from his face, and then he smiles at me. "You're welcome."

Once he's steering the truck down the street, I say, "It was really nice spending the night at your house."

"The offer still stands," he murmurs, his attention on the road ahead. "You can move in this afternoon. I'll go with you to get the rest of your clothes."

Last night I was hesitant, but after this morning, I think it would be nice.

But.

Won't it be weird? I haven't known them that long.

What will people think?

"Don't worry about it now," Colton says as if he can sense my worry.

When he stops the truck in the school's parking area, my eyes go to the entrance of the main building, and I pat nervously over my hair.

"Does it hurt?" Colton asks.

"No, but… ah…" I feel self-conscious for asking but push through, "can you see any of the scabs?"

Colton shakes his head, and lifting a hand, he nudges a strand to the side from where it fell over my right eye. "Not at all. You still look pretty, so don't let anything those assholes say get to you."

I let out a slow breath, then push the door open and climb out. I wait for Colton before we walk to the entrance, and this time I stick close to his side.

I feel eyes on me but keep my head down as I walk to my locker. I'm just about to open it when I see a poster stuck to it.

It takes a moment to realize what I'm looking at, and then the blood chills in my veins.

"Damn, don't you think a dollar is a bit steep for groping?" Michael taunts from behind me.

There's a photo of me taking a shower in the school locker room, with a list of prices for nasty things. My eyes dart over the words, each one digging a chunk out of my heart and soul.

$1 – Groping. $1 – Full Frontal. $1 – Strip Show.

$2 – Handjob. $2 – Blowjob. $1 – Missionary.

$3 – Doggy. $3 – Cowgirl. $3 – Valedictorian.

This isn't happening.

NoNoNoNoNo.

Everyone has written all over it, and someone even wrote **'not my cum'** with an arrow pointing to the suds on my shoulder.

Kill yourself. Hoover lips. Fuggly cunt.

Puked here. Freak. In your dreams. Funny as fuck.

Waste of space. Dick 4 Freak. I'll drown her for free.

It feels like something snaps inside me as humiliation burns through me like hot coals.

Only then does everyone's laughter get through to me.

They all saw it.

My emotions spin out of control, and they begin to suffocate me until all I can hear are my breaths.

"Fuck," Colton snaps, and my eyes dart to his face. He's staring at the poster.

He's seeing all the ugly words and the photo of me – naked from behind.

He sees me just like everyone else does.

An unbearable mortification makes me move away from him.

The last of my will to live fades away, leaving me with one thought only – I need to end this hell.

I turn and break out into a run, needing to get away from the shame and hopeless despair that chases me like a million hell hounds.

My breaths burn over my lips, and my heart pounds against my ribs as I sprint down the stairs. My bag falls to the ground, and I leave it as I race across the parking area.

After last night, I don't have any strength left to process what just happened.

I'm done.

I can't handle it anymore.

I'm going to put an end to this because whatever waits in the afterlife has to be better than this nightmare.

COLTON

Enraged, I yank the paper off Brie's locker, and crumpling it, I shove it into my pocket. I turn to where Michael is laughing his ass off. Not caring about the consequences, my fist connects with his jaw.

He slams into the opposite row of lockers, and the other students move out of the way.

"I'm going to kill you," I growl as I swing another blow at him. I can't hear anything past the bastard's grunts as my fist keeps connecting with his face.

I'm going to fucking kill him.

Hands grab at my arm, but I manage to pull free, delivering another punch to Michael's jaw before they grab hold of me again.

"Let go," I shout, needing to end the piece of shit in front of me.

"That's enough," Mr. Matthews snaps, and it's only then I realize that teachers are here. "To the office! Now!" Mr. Matthews barks.

Knowing I can't risk getting myself expelled, I back off and stalk to the damn office with a bleeding Michael right behind me.

My heart is pounding so damn hard I won't be surprised if it ripped through my chest.

We're ushered into Mr. Davis, the principal's office, and joined by Dr. Montgomery, the school's counselor.

"Someone want to tell me what this is about?" Mr. Davis asks from where he's sitting on the other side of the desk.

I dig the poster out of my pocket and straighten it out before I slam it down in front of him. "He did this to Brie Weinstock."

"You don't have any proof," Michael mutters arrogantly.

"He bullies her every day," I snap, unable to calm down. "What are you going to do about it?"

Mr. Davis' eyes go to Michael. "Wait outside. I'll deal with you later."

Michael lets out a huff and pulls his phone out of his pocket as he walks to the door. He's clearly not worried at all.

Probably because they're not going to do anything.

"You can't beat up another student, no matter what the reason," Mr. Davis says to me.

I glare at the man, my insides boiling. "Just give me my punishment so I can go make sure my friend is okay."

"You need to meet with Dr. Montgomery to talk about that temper of yours."

"Okay."

"Next time you pull a stunt like this, I'm suspending you."

"Fine."

"Get to class."

Not a chance in hell.

I get up, and as I leave the office, I glare at Michael. "We're not done."

"Aww, are you asking me on a date?" Michael taunts me, an egotistical smirk pulling at his bloody lip.

"After school," I mutter.

"Michael, get in here," Mr. Davis calls out.

"Devil's Bluff," Michael says, way too confident after the beating I just gave him.

I hurry out of the building, and pulling my phone out of my pocket, I call Brie's number, but it goes to voicemail. I notice her bag at the foot of the steps and pick it up.

Glancing around the area, I don't see her anywhere, and I rush to my truck. When I climb in, my phone chimes with a message. Seeing it's from Brie, I open it quickly.

Thank you for everything.

My phone vibrates again as another message comes through from her.

I'm sorry.

"No." I start the engine and drive as fast as I can while I keep calling her number. "Don't do this, Brie."

Don't let me be too late.

Fuck, I should've gone after her immediately.

God.

Not again.

Please, not again.

I speed down our street and almost roll the truck when I turn into Brie's driveway. I hope she didn't go somewhere else.

Shit, I don't know what I'll do then.

Luckily the front door isn't locked, and pushing it open, I dart inside. When I reach the foot of the stairs, I hear Brie's mother tauntingly say, "Put me out of my misery and do it already. It will be quick."

I rush up the stairs and follow the sound of Brie's mother's voice. "Just tie it around your neck. You're so goddamn pathetic you can't even do this right."

I dart into the room, and the world is ripped from under my feet when I see a belt tied inside the closet, and Brie's gripping the end of it with both her hands. She's sobbing uncontrollably, and her mother is standing behind her.

"Get out!" I shout, and grabbing hold of the hideous woman, I drag her to the door and shove her so hard she falls into the hallway. I slam the door shut, and when I turn to Brie, her eyes are on me, fear and shame, making her look devastated. "Brie." Her name is nothing but a plea on my lips.

146

"L-l-leave," she stammers through the sobs wracking her.

"No." I move closer, and it makes a pained look flash over her face.

The door slams open, and Brie's bitch of a mother glares at me. "How dare you! I'll call the police."

I walk back to her, and not caring that I'm threatening a woman, I growl, "Call them. We'll show them the cuts on her head and tell them what an abusive bitch you are. I'm sure you'd look great in orange."

My words hit the spot because she steps back from me, sneering, "You're both so damn dramatic. It's not like she'll actually go through with it. God give me strength!"

I shove her out of the room, growling, "Get the fuck out."

I turn back to Brie and see that she's still holding on to the belt. I slowly inch closer until I'm right outside the closet and hold a hand out to Brie. "Please don't. I can help you."

Brie shakes her head. "You s-saw it."

"It doesn't matter." I keep my hand stretched out to her. "Please, Brie."

"It matters to me," she whispers, tightening her grip on the belt.

God, what can I say to make her calm down?

"Remember what we spoke about last night? You have me," I remind her of the moment we shared. "You're not alone anymore."

I see the hesitation in her eyes and take another step forward until I can reach her hands. Wrapping mine around hers, I pull them away from the belt.

Her sobs grow harder as I pull her out of the closet, and the moment I'm able to wrap my arms around her, the suffocating hold that was crushing my heart eases a little.

"I'm so sorry that happened," I say because someone has to apologize to her, and it sure as hell won't be that bastard. I glance at the clothes scattered on the floor and pulling back from Brie, I ask, "Do you have a bag so we can pack your stuff?" She hesitates, and it has me adding, "I'm not leaving you here. You're coming with me."

"But…" she bites her bottom lip, tears still spilling over her cheeks, "I'm a mess."

"Not to me." My words make her eyes dart up to mine. I close the small distance between us, and framing her face, I say, "You're a beautiful girl that's been treated like shit. You deserve better, Brie."

Brie's mom throws a trash bag into the room and sneers, "Pack your shit and get out of my house."

I grab it and begin to stuff clothes into it. It only takes us a couple of minutes because Brie fills an old school bag as well.

When we're done, I grab Brie's hand and drag her out of the room. When we reach the front door, the bitch barks, "What? Not even a goodbye to the woman who raised you."

Brie begins to glance over her shoulder, but I snap, "Don't. She doesn't deserve shit from you."

I toss the bags onto the back of the truck, and once we've climbed inside, I reverse as quickly as I can.

From now on, I'll look after Brie, and God help the person who tries to hurt her again.

It's only when we pull into my driveway that I realize what just happened.

Brie was going to commit suicide, and I managed to stop her.

I stopped her.

The thought shudders through me.

I bring the truck to a standstill and reaching for Brie, I pull her against my chest. I bury my face in her neck and hold onto her for dear life.

I could've saved Brady if only he'd given me the chance.

Chapter 12

BRIE

There are no words to describe the chaos inside of me. It feels like a tornado just swept through me, only leaving devastation and death behind. *The death of the last of my self-esteem.*

Colton holds me for so long that by the time he pulls back, it's like the sun is shining over what's left of the destruction. You can see every piece of debris scattered over an unrecognizable life.

And yet, there's a smile playing around Colton's lips, and as he stares at me, he whispers, "Thank you."

I frown because I don't understand why he'd say that.

"Thank you for letting me help you." His voice is hoarse with emotion, and it makes the lump in my throat swell.

He opens the door and climbs out of the truck, so I do the same. I grab one bag while Colton gets the other, and then I turn to look at the Lawsons' house.

Will this really be home from now on?

Can anywhere feel like home when I'm an outcast?

When we walk inside, Mrs. Lawson turns from where she's washing the dishes and asks, "What happened?"

"I'll tell you in a minute," Colton answers.

Feeling overly self-conscious, I follow Colton up the stairs and into a guestroom. There's a bed and a bedside table, and the walls are painted a generic white. I place the bag next to the one Colton sets down.

Colton walks to the door, and I begin to wonder what I should do now, but instead of him leaving, he shuts it. When he comes to take a seat on the edge of the bed, he pats the space next to him.

I sit down and wring my hands anxiously, sure I'm in trouble after the stunt I pulled.

If only I had the guts to go through with it, everything would be over by now.

"What are you thinking about?" he murmurs.

I swallow hard on the lump in my throat and feeling miserable, I mutter, "I didn't mean to upset you." My insides clench into a tight ball as I admit, "I panicked when you saw the poster. I don't want you looking at me the way the other students do. I thought it would be better just to end it all, but I didn't have the guts to go through with it." I

152

suck in a shaky breath. "And then my mother kept taunting me… and… it was just hard."

There's a moment's silence, then Colton says, "I'm not going to pretend I know the right thing to say, but…" He sucks in a deep breath of air and turns his body toward mine, resting his right knee on the mattress. "Please give me a chance. I promise to try my hardest to make everything okay and to protect you."

He won't always be there, and I can't expect him to either.

"Brie," he whispers. "Please, look at me."

Feeling too ashamed, I can only shake my head. I shut my eyes against the constant bombardment of humiliation and dejection.

I feel Colton move closer, and then his arms wrap around me, and he pulls me to his chest. I'm too battered to put up much of a fight against the threatening tears, and a sob rips through me, robbing me of my breath.

Colton presses a kiss to the side of my head, and then he whispers, "God, Brie. I wish you'd believe me when I say you're not alone anymore. I know the past two days have been shit, but it will get better. I promise."

I pull a little back, and with a trembling hand, I wipe the tears from my face while mumbling, "It's not that I don't believe you."

Colton tilts his head, and there's so much worry and empathy on his face as he asks, "What then?"

"It's just..." I let out an exhausted sigh, "it's too much." My chin begins to tremble again, but I swallow hard, miserably whispering, "And like I said before, it bothers me that you saw it."

"The poster?" Colton's hand settles on my back, and he rubs soothingly over it. "I don't care about shit like that, Brie. I'm just pissed off with that bastard for hurting you again."

I shake my head and needing him to understand, I admit, "You saw me..." I shut my eyes as I force the word out, "naked."

Everyone did.

"Hey," Colton murmurs, and bringing his hands to my face, he nudges me to look at him. It's too hard, and I focus on his neck. "It was only from behind, and besides the fact that Michael is an absolute dick for doing that, you have nothing to be ashamed of."

Not agreeing, I shake my head.

"Brie, you're beautiful." His words are soft and warm, and they make my eyes slowly inch up until I meet his gaze. "Yeah, it sucks that everybody saw you naked but," he shakes his head, and his eyes are intense as they're locked on mine, "at the risk of sounding like a pervert, you have one hell of a hot body."

I can only stare at Colton because no one has ever said anything like that to me.

He thinks I'm pretty. That I'm hot.

Is it out of pity or because he really thinks that?

Still, it revives some of my obliterated self-esteem.

The corner of Colton's mouth lifts. "This is where you slap me for saying something inappropriate."

I shake my head. I'll never be able to hurt him.

"At least tell me to shut up before I keep going and embarrass us both." He scrunches his nose, and it's so cute a smile wavers around my mouth. "Do you feel better?"

I lift my hand and indicate 'a little' with my thumb and pointer finger an inch apart.

"What will make you feel better?"

There's only one thing, and I face plant against him, wrapping my arms tightly around his waist.

Colton holds me, and as he lowers his head, I feel his breaths skim over my neck.

I close my eyes, and even though I'm thoroughly rattled by what happened, I have to admit, I do feel better.

Colton once again saved me. Maybe I should trust him because, so far, he's done nothing to hurt me.

Pressing harder against him, I admit, "I do trust you."

Colton's hold on me tightens, and I feel his lips skim over my skin as he whispers, "Thank you. I won't let you regret it." He pulls back, and bringing his hands to my face, he frames my cheeks. There's a different look darkening his eyes as he stares at me.

Something weird and unexpected begins to grow inside my chest. It's an emotion I haven't felt before – filled with warmth and excitement.

There's a knock at the door, and we instantly pull apart.

Mrs. Lawson peeks into the room. Her eyes fall on the bags at the foot of the bed, and then she smiles. "I'm glad to see you're moving in, Brie."

"Thank you, Mrs. Lawson," I reply, and still feeling uneasy about just moving in, I stand up and ramble, "I'll help with the chores. I promise not to be a burden."

She waves the words away and walks closer. "It will be nice to have another woman in the house."

Colton let's out a chuckle. "Yeah, I'll be outnumbered."

Mrs. Lawson takes another step closer and slowly lifts a hand to my face. I instantly stiffen, bracing for the worst. But then she tenderly brushes the bangs away from my forehead.

"I hope you'll feel right at home with us, and if you need anything, you can tell me," she says.

I nod, and not used to affection, especially from a mother figure, my chin begins to tremble.

Mrs. Lawson slowly pulls me into a hug, and fear makes my heartbeat speed up. I stand frozen as she begins to rub a hand up and down my back.

Then something strange happens, and warmth begins to spread through my chest from her soft touch. Embracing Mrs. Lawson feels so different from hugging Colton.

It becomes more comforting.

It's everything I ever wanted from my mother but never had.

She smells like flowers, and she feels like… a mom.

Overwhelmed by feeling the gentleness of a real mother's touch, tears flood my eyes because it feels so good. It's so soothing.

She doesn't snap at me for being over-emotional. She doesn't accuse me of being dramatic.

She just holds me and continues to rub a gentle hand over my back.

When Mrs. Lawson pulls back, there's a motherly smile on her face, and her eyes shine with unshed tears. She lifts a hand to my hair, and again she brushes the strands away from my eyes. Then she glances around the room. "I think we should go shopping to get a few things for the room. You know, to make it yours."

"Okay." There's a fluttering of excitement in my chest, easing some of the tension I feel.

"Maybe something to hang on the walls? And fairy lights? What's your favorite color? We can get a new bed cover and pillowcases to match then."

My eyes dart over the room, and a million thoughts pop into my head. Still too overwhelmed, I can't voice any of them, so instead, I mumble, "Anything will be great."

"We can make it a fun project." Then she grows serious. "Is it okay if I ask you a couple of questions?"

I nod and nervously clasp my hands together. Colton just sits on the bed watching us, but knowing he's here makes me feel safe.

"You're a senior, right?"

"Yes, I'll be eighteen soon."

There's relief on her face as she says, "That's good news. When's your birthday?"

"September twenty-third."

Her mouth curves into a smile again. "Oh, Colton is October twenty-third. It's an easy date to remember." Then she adds, "It's in two weeks. We'll do something special and go shopping for everything then."

I smile at the idea because I've never celebrated it before.

"What did your mother say when you left?"

The question makes the smile drop from my face. Ashamed, I answer, "Ah... she told me to leave."

Mrs. Lawson's eyebrows dart up, but then she schools her face, hiding the surprise. "Maybe that's for the best, then she won't try to fight us for you."

Her comment makes anxiety worm it's way back into my chest. "I don't want to cause you and Colton any trouble."

Mrs. Lawson waves her hand. "You're no trouble at all. I just want to be prepared, but with you turning eighteen soon, you'll be an adult, so I'm sure even if she did make a fuss, everything would work out fine."

The encouraging words make me feel a little less apprehensive.

"I'll leave you to get settled." Mrs. Lawson gives me another sideways squeeze before she leaves.

Even though the morning was a nightmare, I really do feel better after all the comfort Colton and his mom has given me.

It makes hope find its way back into my heart again that the future might be brighter and that everything will work out okay.

Chapter 13

COLTON

When Mom leaves the room, I glance up to Brie. Michael's been in the back of my mind all morning. Now that I'm calmer, I feel it will be a waste of my time meeting him. Some idiots just can't be reasoned with.

"There's something we need to talk about," I say, patting the space next to me again. After she takes a seat, I suck in a deep breath, not knowing how Brie is going to react. "I have to meet Michael at Devil's Bluff after school."

Her eyes widen on me. "Why?"

"After you left this morning, I got into a fight with him."

A worried look settles on Brie's face, and then she asks, "Did you get in trouble?"

"I got off with a warning. But afterward... I was pissed off and agreed to meet Michael so we can settle this shit."

"But…" Brie's eyebrows knit together, "you don't have to."

I shake my head. "We both have to go, Brie. We have to make a statement, so they'll stop bullying you."

Her shoulders slump, and she lets out a tired sigh. "But I don't want you getting into fights because of me."

"One fight." I hold up my pointer finger. "That's all it will take."

Her eyes drift over my face before they lower back to her hands. "But what if you get hurt?"

The fact that she's worried about me makes my heart tighten and expand at the same time.

"I've had a lot of practice. Michael won't get the chance to hurt me," I state.

Brie pulls her bottom lip between her teeth, and it draws my undivided attention to her mouth.

I wonder if she's ever been kissed.

Get your mind out of the gutter. You have the fight to focus on, or you will get your ass kicked.

"I'll be okay," I reassure her. I take hold of her hand and hold it between both of mine. "You need to see how to stand up for yourself. I'll always try to be there, but I want you to learn how to handle these assholes."

She shakes her head, and after a couple of seconds, mutters, "They won't ever listen to me."

"You have to make them listen," I say.

Brie pulls her hand from mine, and she looks so tired that I say, "You don't have to do anything now. I just want to show you how to deal with them."

Reluctantly, Brie nods.

"We should get going. Do you know where Devil's Bluff is?" I ask.

Brie nods again, and we get up from the bed.

"Let me just tell my mom we're heading out." I walk to Mom's room, and not finding her there, a grin spreads over my face.

I catch up to Brie, where she's waiting outside her room. "She's probably downstairs."

We find Mom in the kitchen. She has the fridge open, frowning.

"We're just going somewhere. Do you need me to stop at the store?"

Mom shuts the fridge. "Yes, can you get some eggs and milk?"

"Sure."

Brie waves at my mom, and then we walk out to the truck. Once settled in the cab, she says, "It's on the outskirts of town. I haven't gone there much."

I steer the vehicle down the street. "Show the way."

The area grows thicker with trees as we near the first lookout point.

"I've heard students like to come here to make out," Brie mutters. "There's also a waterfall with a pool where they usually party if you follow that trail."

I stop a distance from the other cars, so I don't get blocked in. My eyes go over the already forming crowd as I unbutton the cuffs of my school shirt. Rolling up my sleeves, I say, "Just stay behind me."

"Do I have to go with you?" Brie asks, apprehension evident in her voice.

She's had a tough day, and the last thing I want to do is add to it.

"No, you can stay here and watch."

Brie lets out a breath of air.

I reach for her hand and give it a squeeze. "I'll be right back."

Climbing out of the truck, I stalk toward an arrogantly grinning Michael.

"Finally," he calls out. "I thought you were going to chicken out." I don't reply, and as I near Michael, he says, "Two hits. My fist hitting your jaw and you hitting the ground."

When I'm close enough, I throw everything into the punch, and Michael drops like a sack of potatoes. He groans in pain as he struggles to turn onto his side.

"Next time you fuck with Brie, I'll kill you," I growl. My gaze darts over the other students. "The same goes for all of you. Leave her the fuck alone."

I turn around and walk to the truck. I slide in behind the steering wheel and say, "That's how it's done."

I start the engine and glare at where Michael has managed to sit up. He shakes his head, and when our eyes meet, there's no sign of the arrogance he always wears like a damn cloak.

Next time I'll break his damn jaw.

The tires kick up dirt as I pull away, and then Brie murmurs, "I'm glad you're on my side."

Our eyes meet for a moment, and as I turn my attention back to the road, I whisper, "Always."

After stopping at the store, we head home. I set the bag with the milk and eggs on the kitchen table and look at the flour and other ingredients spread out on the counter.

"What are you making?" I ask Mom.

"A cake," she grins happily. "I figured we should celebrate Brie moving in."

"Great idea," I agree, especially because Mom hasn't baked since we moved here. "I hope it's chocolate."

"Of course," Mom gives me a playful smile. "I wouldn't dare make anything else."

I go to press a kiss to Mom's cheek and whisper, "I missed this. Thank you." Pulling back, I say, "We're going to unpack Brie's clothes."

"Brie," Mom calls as we begin to walk away, "will you make a list of everything you need?" Mom signals something with her eyes. "You know, personal stuff."

Ugh.

I roll my eyes but then can't stop the chuckle when I see Brie's face redden with a blush as she nods frantically.

Walking into Brie's room, I say, "Let's get you settled in."

Brie grabs the smaller bag and begins to shove her underwear into the back of the closet. She's cute, and I have to suppress my laughter because I don't want to embarrass her.

I open the other bag and throw the clothes out on the bed. Picking up a shirt, I hang it in the closet before turning back to the bundle.

After a couple of minutes, I catch Brie staring at me, a smile softening her features.

"What?" I ask, the corners of my mouth lifting.

"I just realized I have a friend," she admits.

I grin at her before grabbing another shirt. It's been a lousy morning, but at least something good came from it – she's here, and she trusts me. Oh, and I got to kick Michael's ass. Hopefully, the bastard will back off now.

I glance at Brie again, and my eyes drop to her unflattering uniform. After seeing that photo of her naked, it's hard not to recall what she looked like.

I wasn't lying earlier when I told her she's hot.

That's actually an understatement. I might've only seen her naked from behind, but it was enough for me to know she has a body meant for wet dreams.

Don't be a pervert, asshole.

I shake my head and grab another item of clothing. Still, it's becoming impossible to ignore the attraction I feel toward her. Especially now that we're friends and she doesn't get anxious around me.

With all the shit that happened in my own life, I haven't dated the past year and a half. I didn't have the energy for it.

But now…

My eyes drift to Brie again, and I take in her delicate features and hypnotizing blue eyes. My gaze drops to her mouth.

This girl is nothing short of perfect.

How has no one seen that yet?

All the idiots at school must be blind as fuck.

Brie glances at the remaining clothes, and then she catches me staring at her. "Is something wrong?"

I tilt my head and gather the guts to ask, "Have you dated before?"

"Huh?" Her eyes widen, and then she looks confused as if she can't comprehend why I'd ask her a question like that. "Like, had a boyfriend?"

I nod. "Yeah."

She shakes her head then crouches to grab another pair of shorts. "I'm an outcast. Guys don't date girls like me."

I pull a what-the-fuck face. "That's bullshit."

Brie shrugs my words away and mumbles, "Besides, I'm too awkward."

"No, you're not," I argue. "Yeah, you don't talk much, and you're withdrawn, but that's not a bad thing."

The corner of her mouth lifts a little. "I always thought you were quiet as well."

I grin at her. "Are you trying to tell me in a nice way that I talk too much?"

Brie lets out a nervous chuckle. "No, not at all." A blush begins to creep up her neck as she admits, "When I first saw you, I thought you'd be a bully." She makes an awkward gesture with her hand. "It was the nose ring and earrings." Looking thoroughly uncomfortable, she continues, "And when you walk, it looks like you're prowling for a victim."

My grin keeps growing, and my heartbeat excitedly speeds up. I can't resist teasing her, "Hmm, so you think I'm badass."

"Ahh…" A breath sputters from her, and the blush spreads to her cheeks. "It's not that I think you're bad." I can see it's hard for her to express her thoughts, so I patiently keep quiet. Brie sucks in a deep breath, then mumbles, "You're kind and don't take crap from anyone, and…" her movements become jittery as if she's nervous.

169

Then she rambles, "If I ever get to date a guy, I hope he's like you."

That's seriously the last thing I expected Brie to say. She begins to work faster while I'm still staring at her with surprise.

What the hell do I reply to that?

Let's date?

Hell no, Brie needs to get used to being a part of a family before she can deal with something as complicated as a relationship.

But I don't want to leave her hanging either because I know how fragile her self-esteem is.

Shit. I also don't want to miss my chance, and then some other idiot snatches her up.

My heart is nothing but a nervous drumming in my chest.

"Well," I wet my lips and trying to be nonchalant about it all, I mumble, "let me know when you're ready to date."

The frown deepens on her forehead, and she hesitantly glances at me. "Uh… why?"

Damn, this conversation is challenging.

I shrug, pretending to be cool about it. *Which I'm definitely not.* "Once everything is better, we can maybe go on… a date."

"Yeah?" Brie rubs her palms over the fabric of her skirt.

"Yeah. Sure." I swallow hard, and it feels like I'm going to overheat.

The prom is still months away, but if I ask her now, then at least she won't say yes to someone else, and it will give her plenty of time to settle in. "Like the prom?"

She wets her lips nervously, then whispers, "Uhm... Okay."

An awkward as hell silence falls between us, and we work fast to finish putting all the clothes away. When we're done, I walk to the door and mutter, "Let's get something to drink."

"Okay."

When we walk into the kitchen where Mom's stirring the cake mixture, I let out a relieved breath.

"Can we help?" I ask.

Mom smiles at me. "I'm just about to put the cake in the oven. Would you mind making dinner later? I was hoping for steak, mash potatoes, and green beans. It was delicious the last time you made them."

"Sure." I walk to the freezer and remove three steaks, so they have time to defrost.

Mom glances at Brie. "Did you make the list, dear?"

171

"Uhm, no." Brie begins to backpedal. "I'll go make it quickly. Sorry." She rushes back up the stairs.

I glance at Mom and whisper, "She'll get better."

Mom nods. "Yeah, she just needs time."

I lean back against the counter and watch as Mom pours the mixture into a cake pan. "How are you?"

Mom shoots me a quizzical look. "I'm fine."

"I mean, since Brie's been here, you've been out of bed more."

A soft smile forms around her lips. "I just want to be there for Brie. She's had a rough go at life." Mom shrugs.

"So you're really okay with her living here?"

"Of course." Mom hesitates, and then her voice drops to a sad whisper, "Maybe I can be a mom for her, and she…"

My eyes are locked on her. "Mom, Brie won't be able to fill the gap Brady left."

"I know," she signs sorrowfully. "But it helps."

"Yeah," I agree. "It helps."

A lot.

I know I have to tell my mom about Brie's suicide attempt, but it's only been a little over three months since Brady passed away, and I'm scared it will break her.

"So, you feel okay?" I ask her again.

Mom sets the spoon down and turns to me. "Yes, I know things have been tough, but it's slowly getting better."

I clear my throat and suck in a deep breath. "At school, an idiot made a poster. It had a photo of Brie showering. She took it really hard and…" God, this is hard. I watch Mom's reaction carefully.

"Kids can be so cruel," Mom snaps, obviously unhappy hearing Brie was bullied.

"Yeah," I agree with her. "Ah… Mom…" I move closer to her and place my hand on her shoulder. "Brie ran home, and by the time I got there, she was… considering suicide, but I managed to stop her." Wanting to spare my mom the heartache, I don't go into the details.

Mom's hands visibly tremble, and her eyes begin to shine. I pull her into a hug wanting to comfort her.

After a moment, Mom whispers, "But Brie's okay now?"

"She'll get there. It's going to take time."

Mom pulls back and places a hand against my cheek. "I know I've been a shitty mom, but I want you to know how proud I am of you. You have such a good heart."

"Got that from you," I tease her.

"I love you," Mom says. I haven't heard the words in a while, and they fill my chest with warmth.

"Love you, too."

Brie walks back into the kitchen, and Mom says, "Oh, sweetheart. Colton just told me what happened this morning. I'm so sorry."

Brie's eyes drop to the floor, and she shrugs. "It's… okay."

"Whoever did that to you is just petty and mean," Mom continues.

Brie nods and seeing how uncomfortable she is with this conversation, I ask, "Do you want some coke?"

Brie moves closer to me, her eyes continually darting to my mom. "Please."

While I pour us each a glass, I think how it's only been twenty-four hours since Brie walked into this house, and already everything has changed.

At first, it was a desperate hope that Brie would give my mom a new reason to live, but now I know she will.

Brie might need us, but we needed her more.

Chapter 14

BRIE

I feel nauseous as Colton and I walk into school.

Everyone's eyes are on us again, but no one says anything, and there's no sign of Michael.

"I hear you and Michael had a fight," Sully suddenly says behind us. "One punch, hey?"

Sully throws his arm around Colton's shoulders, but Colton immediately shrugs it off and growls, "Don't touch me."

"So damn sensitive, dude," Sully says with his hands up to indicate peace, then his eyes fall on me. "Damn, Weinstock. What happened to your hair?"

Before he can say anything else, Colton shoves him away, snarling, "Don't talk to her. I'll rearrange your face if you so much as glance at Brie. Stay the fuck away from us."

The grin fades from Sully's face, and then he glares at us before he stalks off.

Colton turns to me. "That's how you deal with a bully. They're cowards by nature and will only engage if they think it's a sure win. You might have to snap at them a couple of times, but they'll get the message and leave you alone."

Yeah, right. No amount of snapping from me will get the bullies to back off.

I don't say anything as Colton wraps his arm around my shoulder and pulls me into his side when we begin to walk again.

I have to admit it feels… safe, walking next to Colton, and it makes the corner of my mouth lift slightly.

———————

When I have to go to PE without Colton, I duck my head low and start sending up prayers no one will notice me.

I keep close to the wall as I move through the throng of students, and rounding a corner, I slam into someone. My eyes dart up, and seeing that it's another student, Carter, anxiety spikes through me like a rocket. He's not a bully per se, but he's known for being violent.

"Out of my way," he growls, shoving me hard against the wall.

I stand frozen as Carter passes by, but he doesn't make it far before Dr. Montgomery, the school's counselor, grabs hold of his arm, dragging him to the classroom alcove near the girls' locker rooms.

I hang back, not wanting to get in the way while she talks to him. It's clear they're both upset.

When Carter storms off a few moments later, not looking my way, I decide it's safe enough to move. The warning bell rings, and gripping my sketchpad tighter to my chest, I walk faster.

"Hey. Wait," I hear Dr. Montgomery call, but figure she's calling after Carter.

Just before I can slip inside the locker room, someone grabs hold of my shoulder. I let out a frightened squeak but seeing it's Dr. Montgomery, I let out a sigh of relief.

"Hey, what's your name?"

Crap, the last thing I need right now is the school's counselor wanting to talk with me. I worry my bottom lip, and keeping my eyes on the floor, I mutter, "Brie."

"Brie, you should come talk to me soon."

I glance up and down the hallway, wondering what I should reply with.

"Hey," she lowers her voice, "No one has to know. Just come see me. Okay? I promise it will be our secret."

Yeah, right. The last time I went to a counselor because my mother broke my arm, they called child protection services, and a woman came to our house. It only caused me a world of trouble.

Never again.

I nod so she'll leave me alone and then dart into the locker room.

Ugh, I wish I could have all my classes with Colton. Everything is just so much easier when he's around.

COLTON

Walking into the cafeteria, I don't see Brie. I stand in line and get myself pizza, then go sit at a table near the back, making sure I can see the entrance and queue from where I am.

Brie instantly catches my eye when she darts into the room. Her shoulders are hunched, and her eyes are glued to the floor.

She quickly grabs something to eat, then walks in my direction. Her gaze stops on the table she always sits at, but then she keeps walking, and I can't help but grin as she comes to sit down next to me.

"You okay?" I ask, glancing at the spaghetti on her tray.

"Yeah."

Some guys holler at a nearby table, and Brie freezes, her eyes snapping to them.

"Tell me who's who at this school," I say, hoping to draw her into a conversation.

She gestures to the noisy table. "They're in a band. Trigger. I've heard it's popular. That's Cole Travis. The others are Tristan and Benjamin. Michael's also in the band."

I stare at the group. "So, they're Michael's friends."

"I don't know. It doesn't look like Cole and Michael get along." Brie gestures to a girl walking by our table. "That's Keira Sheppard. She's nice."

A guy walks into the cafeteria, and Brie mumbles, "Nathaniel Black. His family practically owns the school, and he's head of the swim team." Then she gestures to another group of guys. "That's the football team."

Brie's eyes scan over the rest of the students, and then they stop on me. "I'm glad you're here. It sucked watching new people walk in at the beginning of the year, and they all just fit in. It made me wonder what I was doing wrong that I could never fit in anywhere."

Damn, I want to hug her right now.

Instead, I grin. "Yeah, now you're stuck with me."

The most beautiful smile spreads over her face, and then she twirls some spaghetti around her fork. It reminds me of the pizza on my plate. We both take a couple of bites of our meals, then Brie points to the book I'm reading; *Between a Rock and a Hard Place by Aaron Ralston.* "When I first saw you, I didn't take you for a reader." She licks her lips, then adds, "Then again, I've been wrong about everything where you're concerned."

"I just started it. It's good."

"Have you always loved reading?"

I shake my head. "It's a new hobby." I take another bite of my lunch and first swallow before I ask, "Do you have any hobbies?"

Brie points to her sketchpad that's lying next to her plate. "Just drawing."

"Right." Wondering what else she's drawn, I ask, "Mind if I look at the sketches?"

Brie hesitates, her eyes turning to the book. "Ah… okay." She picks it up and moves it closer to me.

I shove the plate away and first wipe my hands clean on a napkin before opening the book. "A person wading through water," I murmur. Brie nods, the corner of her mouth lifting nervously. I turn the page. "The screaming girl. I've seen this one."

"You have?" She looks surprised.

"Yeah." I lock eyes with her. "Is the picture you?"

Her gaze flits away before she nods.

Turning the page, the air is knocked from my lungs. The picture is different from the others.

"That's me in five years," Brie admits.

"Yeah?" I murmur, captivated by how she sees herself. Butterflies flutter from a girl that's looking up.

Brie always had hope.

"It's beautiful…" I turn my gaze back to Brie, "just like you."

She grins shyly, then confesses, "That's how I feel now that I'm living with you."

Screw what everyone thinks. I wrap an arm around Brie's shoulders and pull her into my side. Pressing a kiss to her temple, I murmur, "It makes me happy hearing that."

I don't let go of her as I turn the page, but the next one is blank. "What are you going to draw next?"

"I don't know." She pulls her bottom lip between her teeth as she thinks about it. "Maybe something abstract. I need to have more for a portfolio if I want to apply to art school."

"You still have time," I remind her.

She glances up at me and then says, "I can always draw you."

I let out a chuckle. "Go for it. I'd like to see what you come up with."

Brie takes another bite of her food, then pushes the plate to the side, asking, "Can I ask you something?"

"Sure."

She rests an elbow on the table and leans her cheek against her palm. I do the same, and it brings our faces close together, but I don't pull back.

"Why did you give me those quotes?"

Sitting so near to her, I can see a dark blue ring around the lighter blue of the iris.

Hypnotizing eyes, for sure.

My voice is low as I answer, "Seeing Michael bully you made me so damn angry. I wanted you to fight back."

"You haven't given me any since the text message," she whispers.

It feels as if we're in our own little bubble. I like it.

"I got the impression they bothered you." She's about to say something, but I quickly add, "I understand why, though. I was hard on you, and I'm sorry. I didn't know how bad things were and got frustrated because –" My words cut off when I think of Brady, and there's a familiar pang of sorrow.

"Because?"

"You reminded me of my brother, Brady."

Realization flits over her face. "I'm sorry."

I shake my head and let out a soft chuckle, "It turns out you're much stronger than I gave you credit for."

She lets out a huff. "I'm not strong at all."

I wish Brie could see herself through my eyes. She'd know how special she is.

"You are. The shit you had to survive…" I shake my head, and lifting my other hand, I wrap my fingers around the back of her neck.

Damn, her skin is soft.

"Not many people would be able to handle that. My brother couldn't, and he didn't have to deal with half the abuse you got."

There's a sad smile wavering around her mouth. "What was he like?"

The corner of my mouth lifts slightly. "Brady was sensitive and kind. He was the opposite of me."

"You're kind," she states, her tone firmer than it usually is.

"I wasn't always," I admit. "Before Brady's death, I didn't have time for anyone. I focused all my energy on keeping him safe."

Brie nods, and then she whispers, "Kinda like you're doing with me now."

I let out a burst of air. "Yeah, I guess I'm a one person at a time guy."

Brie's eyes dart to the table before she brings them back to me. She hesitates but then says, "I'm glad I'm that person."

Our gazes lock, and an intense feeling fills the bubble we're caught in. It makes anticipation tighten my chest until my heart is slamming against my ribs.

I wish I could kiss her.

The bell rings, making the bubble pop, and we both pull back at the same time.

Stupid damn bell.

We gather out books and take the trays back before walking out of the cafeteria.

Chapter 15

BRIE

Mrs. Lawson made meatloaf for dinner, and I have to admit it's way better than the cafeteria's.

We had cake for dessert again, and I wish I could ask Mrs. Lawson to teach me how to make one, but I don't have the guts.

Instead, I gather the plates and pile the cutlery on top. Carrying the dishes to the sink, a knife slips off and clatters on the floor.

Oh, crap!

My heart sinks to my stomach, and my hands begin to tremble with anxiety. It makes the other cutlery rattle on the plates, and when a fork falls, my mouth goes bone dry with fear.

NoNoNoNo.

'Now, look what you made me do. You retarded bitch. I swear, the next time a glass breaks in this house, I'll feed you the damn pieces.'

"Brie."

'I should've drowned you at birth. Now, I'm stuck with you. You're pathetic.'

"Brie."

When someone takes the rattling plates from my hands, I begin to cower backward. My eyes fly wildly around the kitchen while my breaths explode over my lips.

"I'm sorry," I whimper. "I didn't mean to."

Suddenly arms wrap around me, and my body freezes with terror. It feels like something tears a gaping hole right through my chest, and I cry, "No!"

"It's okay, sweetheart," Mrs. Lawson murmurs right by my ear. "It's okay."

An agonizing sob escapes, and I manage to yank free from the hold she has on me. Terrified, I stumble backward. My breaths come too fast, and soon, it's hard to get any air in.

I can't focus on anything until Colton moves in front of me. He holds a hand up between us. "Brie, it's okay. You're safe."

I gasp for air and can't stop the sob from escaping my lips.

Colton slowly moves closer, and it takes a moment for the realization to reach me that he won't hurt me.

When Colton takes hold of my shoulder, I bring my hands up and cover my face. The breaths I suck in are painful. Colton wraps his arms around me and gently presses me to his chest.

"It's okay. You're safe," he repeats.

"I'm… sorry," I stammer through the tears, not quite sure what I'm apologizing for. I just know I have to.

Colton pulls back and framing my face with his hands, he presses a kiss to my forehead and uses his thumbs to wipe my tears away. "It was an accident. Okay?"

I nod, and I try to swallow the tears, but it only makes my throat cramp up.

Colton keeps wiping the tears away until I finally manage to stop them, then he smiles at me. "Do you feel better?"

A lost sob drifts over my lips as I nod.

Then Mrs. Lawson says, "I think you should take a nice, long relaxing bubble bath."

Instantly fear pours back through my veins, and I cower closer to Colton.

"I'll take her," Colton says, and holding my hand, he pulls me out of the kitchen and up the stairs.

When we're in the bathroom, I watch as he turns on the faucets and squirts bubble bath into the water.

I watch the waterline rise, and then my eyes nervously dart to him.

When the tub is filled, and steam twirls into the air, I can only stare.

My mother would've drowned me if I dared use so much water.

"Soak for as long as you want, okay," Colton says, his voice soft and kind.

I glance at the water before looking at him, then mumble, "Really? For as long as I want? Your mom won't get upset?"

I don't want to get in trouble.

"She won't. If it turns cold before you're done, just let some out and fill it up with warm water again."

I press my lips together when tears threaten to overwhelm me again. My heart squeezes into a tiny lump to make space for the overwhelming appreciation I feel.

Colton comes to stand in front of me and tilts his head until he catches my eyes. "There's no time limit to how long you're allowed to bathe."

I nod and swallow hard in an attempt to keep the tears back.

He presses a kiss to my forehead, and I close my eyes to soak in the warm feeling.

189

When Colton steps out of the bathroom, shutting the door behind him, I take a moment to just breathe through the panic, still whirling in my chest.

Once I feel calmer, I strip out of my school uniform and step into the balmy water. I lie back, and my eyes drift closed.

I feel guilty over how I reacted when Mrs. Lawson tried to hug me, but I couldn't help it. I know she's the opposite of my mother, and I'll have to try harder to stay calm around her.

My thoughts turn to Colton, and the corners of my mouth lift slightly. He's shown me more kindness over the past three days than I've experienced in my entire life.

It's like he's my own guardian angel.

All my dreams have always been focused years from now because that's how long I thought it would take to get away from my mother.

But they're coming true much sooner.

With the smile widening on my face, I gather some bubbles and blow them into the air.

Then new dreams begin to grow deep in my heart.

Hopefully, the awkwardness between Mrs. Lawson and me will fade. Maybe she can teach me how to cook and bake. She can show me all the things my mother never did.

And maybe… maybe Colton can be my first kiss.

I grin like an idiot while a blush reddens my face. I splash water onto my heated skin.

I quickly wash, but I'm careful when I massage shampoo into my hair. At least the scabs don't burn anymore. When I'm done, I let the water out, and drying myself, I glance around for clean clothes, but then I remember I didn't bring any.

Shoot.

I dry my hair thoroughly, then comb through it with my fingers. Wrapping a towel tightly around my body, I grip it with one hand so it won't accidentally come loose.

Opening the door, I peek into the hallway, and not seeing anyone, I tip-toe out. I'm almost to my room when Colton comes out of his.

The moment his eyes land on me, we both freeze.

"Ahh…" I dart toward my room. "Sorry, I forgot to bring clothes to the bathroom." I dash inside and slam the door shut, then lean back against it while my heart bounces around in my chest.

COLTON

Grinning, I watch Brie run into her room.

That's the last thing I expected to see, but damn, the guy in me won't deny it was one hell of a hot sight.

Up until a second ago, I was worried because of the panic attack Brie had in the kitchen, and now I'm practically wiping drool from my mouth.

Never a dull moment, that's for sure.

I shoot back into my room, and grabbing clean clothes, I go shower quickly. When I'm clean and dressed in my usual sweatpants and t-shirt, I notice Brie's door is open, and she's not in her room.

I hear Mom chuckle from her own room and head in that direction. Standing in the doorway, I watch as Mom squirts something into Brie's palm.

"Just rub it all over your face and neck," Mom says.

I lean a shoulder against the doorjamb and ask, "Brie, you want to watch a movie once you're done?"

She glances over her shoulder. "Sure."

Even though I'm worried about Brie, I know hovering around her won't help her heal. Reluctantly, I leave the women to do their thing. I know the time they spend together is good for both of them.

I go to the living room and sitting down on a couch, I switch on the TV and begin to scroll through the movie selection.

I have no idea what Brie likes to watch, but luckily I don't have to wait long for her. She's aiming for the other couch, but I catch her hand and pull her down next to me.

Mom goes to get a glass of water, then says, "Enjoy the movie. I'm heading to bed. Don't stay up too late."

"Night," I call out.

"Goodnight, Mrs. Lawson," Brie says, and then she looks at me. "What are we watching?"

"I have no idea," I admit. "What kind of movies do you like?"

I scroll through a couple, and when Brie doesn't answer me, I glance at her. She's drawn her bottom lip between her teeth again, then admits, "I don't know what I like."

Oh, right. She wasn't allowed to watch TV, and the way she reacted when Mom said she should take a long bath tells me that was an issue with Brie's mom as well. It must've been hell growing up with that woman for a mother.

Not wanting anything intense, I go to the fantasy and sci-fi section, then ask, "How about The Host. It's about aliens taking over the planet."

"Okay."

I press play, and we watch the first couple of minutes. A soft scent drifts from Brie, and it makes me highly aware of her.

I clear my throat and ask, "Do you feel better?"

She wipes imaginary fluff off her pants, then mutters, "Yeah, sorry. I don't know why that happened earlier."

Lifting an arm, I rest it over her shoulders. "Was it a flashback?"

She nods, and I pull her into my side.

"It happened to me the other day at school," I admit, hoping it will make her feel better.

"It did?" she asks, glancing up at me.

"Yeah. In history."

A light frown forms on her forehead. "Was that when Mr. Donati asked if you're okay?"

"Yeah."

She hesitates, then asks, "What was the flashback about?"

I've never talked to anyone about the abuse we suffered at my father's hands, and it feels awkward. "The first time my father beat me."

A sad expression tightens Brie's features. "I'm sorry it happened to you."

I shrug, not knowing what to say to that. Wondering why she doesn't ask me why I didn't stop him from beating me, I ask, "Aren't you going to ask why I didn't stop him?"

She shakes her head. "I know the reason." My brow furrows, and it has her explaining, "It's easier said than done. The fear they instill in us overrides everything."

I think about what Brie just said, then reply, "That wasn't it in my case. I didn't fight back, because being indifferent used to piss him off even more. I didn't want to give him the satisfaction of knowing he was getting to me. It was a catch twenty-two situation. The more indifferent I became, the more violent he got."

Movement from her hands catches my eye, and remembering the bandage she wore the other day, and now seeing the almost healed cuts, I ask, "What happened to your hand?" I reach for her palm and softly caress my pointer finger over the marks.

"My mom broke a glass, and I was picking up the pieces." Brie pauses for a moment, then continues, "She squeezed my hand closed over the shards because she wanted a reaction from me."

Brie's eyes snap up to mine as if she just realized something. "I guess I did the same thing with my mom. I didn't give her the satisfaction of getting a reaction, and it used to infuriate her. She always called me out for being a zombie and pathetic."

Brie sucks in a deep breath, then admits, "That's what my flashback was about."

A guilty pang fills my chest. Before I got to know Brie, I used to call her out for just taking the bullying. All the while, she was just indifferent in her own way.

Not watching the movie anymore, I turn the volume down a bit, then ask, "Do you want to lie down?"

Brie shifts nervously. "Won't your mom mind?"

I let out a chuckle. "Only if we get naked." Once the words are out, I instantly regret them. "Shit, sorry, that was inappropriate."

Brie just shrugs, then mutters, "We can lie down. I don't mind."

We shift our bodies on the couch, and Brie rests her head on my chest.

After a moment, she mumbles, "Today was nice."

"Yeah?" Seeing as we're not watching TV, I switch it off, and only the light from the kitchen shines into the living room.

"Especially lunch," Brie adds. "It's really nice having a friend."

It is. I never had any because it would risk our family's secret getting out. Brady, on the other hand, had friends and a girlfriend. I wish I knew what he thought when he committed suicide. Then I remember what Brie said. She panicked because I saw the poster.

I hate bringing up the subject, but needing to understand my brother, I ask, "If I hadn't seen the poster, would you still have tried to commit suicide?"

"Huh?" Her head snaps up, and an awkward look shutters her eyes. "Ah... I don't know. Why do you ask?"

Pushing an arm under my head, I stare up at the ceiling. "I wish I knew why my brother did it. He didn't leave a note." Not wanting to talk more about that night, I change the subject. "Have you thought about how you want to decorate your room?"

Brie shakes her head but then says, "I have a million ideas."

"Do you want to paint the walls a different color?"

She thinks for a moment, then says, "Maybe just the one wall. A light blue would be nice."

"I'll help. We can spend your birthday redecorating your room."

There's a moment's silence, and then Brie whispers, "Colton."

"Yeah?"

Her arm wraps around my waist, and she gives me a squeeze before she snuggles into my side. "You're the best thing that's ever happened to me."

Her words make a huge smile spread over my face. Lifting my head, I press a kiss to her hair. "I'm glad I found you in time."

"Me too," she murmurs.

I lie awake as Brie drifts off to sleep, and only once it's me and my thoughts do I admit to myself that I have a crush on her. But I know it will take a little luck and a lot of patience before I can ask her to be my girlfriend. In the meantime, I'll be the best friend she's ever had.

Chapter 16

BRIE

Mom: Stop throwing a tantrum and get your ass home.

I woke up to the message waiting on my phone and have been staring at it for a couple of minutes, not knowing what to reply.

My heart is stuck in my throat, and I'm filled with familiar apprehension.

I still have to get changed for school, but can't bring myself to move. There's a soft tap on my door, and my head snaps up. "Yes?"

"Can I come in?" Colton asks.

"Yeah." I get up from the bed, my gaze darting back to the phone in my hand.

Colton comes in and asks, "Why aren't you dressed?"

I hold the device out to him. "I don't know what to reply with."

He takes the phone and reads the message. "Oh, that's easy. You don't reply and just delete the message."

He hands the device back to me, and my gaze darts between his eyes and the message. "But... it will make her angry."

Colton places a hand on the side of my neck, giving me an encouraging smile. "Brie, she's already pissed off, and it doesn't matter. She doesn't have a say in your life anymore."

I still feel apprehensive but also realize Colton is right. I'm living with them now, and there's nothing my mother can do about it.

"Unless you want to reply," Colton adds.

I shake my head. "No."

I suck in a fortifying breath and read the message one last time before I delete it.

When I glance up at Colton, there's a proud smile on his face. "Get ready, or we'll be late."

I nod, and as soon as he leaves the room, I quickly change into my uniform.

It feels weird living with the Lawsons'. Like it's not my house. It's also frequently in the back of my mind that they might tell me to leave at any time. Kinda like I'm on vacation with them, and one day I'll have to return to my mother.

My eyes dart to my phone, and I regret deleting the message. I should respond.

What if things go wrong here? Where will I go then?

I draw my bottom lip between my teeth, and trepidation tightens my insides.

Colton wouldn't do that to me. Right?

Ugh, this is really hard. What do I do? I really don't want to go back to my mother.

Maybe I should get a job.

My eyes widen at the thought.

Yeah, I'll get a job, and then if things go wrong, I can maybe find a place of my own.

Deciding to look for work after school, I feel a little better and leave my room. When I reach the front door, Colton presses a kiss to his mom's cheek.

With a quick wave, I dart out of the house.

On the way to school, Colton mutters, "It's finally Friday."

"Yeah," I agree. "This week was super long."

"Do you want to do anything tonight?" Colton asks.

This will be the first weekend I won't have to deal with my mother, and the thought alone makes my blood rush through my veins with exhilaration. "Anything is good."

"Want to show me around town?" he asks. "I've been here for three months, and I only know where the store and school are."

"Okay," I agree, excited to spend time with Colton. I'll also be able to see if there are any job vacancies in town.

After Colton parks the truck, we walk into school, and it's the same as yesterday. Students stare, but no one says anything.

We take our seats in English, and minutes later, Colton drops a piece of paper on my desk. Opening it, a wide smile spreads over my face.

'It is never too late to be what you might have been.' – George Eliot.

I glance at Colton and mouth the words 'thank you.'

Knowing he meant well by giving me the quotes, I have to admit I missed them.

As the day progresses, there's no sight of Sully and Michael. I find myself relaxing a little and not feeling as anxious.

That is until Lindy and her friends corner me at my locker before social studies.

"Dang, just when I thought you couldn't look gloomier," she taunts me.

My muscles tense, and I glance at Colton as he walks closer after shutting his own locker.

He glares at Lindy before turning his eyes to me. "Tell her to go to hell."

Crap.

Okay.

I suck in a deep breath for courage.

Before I can think of anything to say, Lindy sneers, "Should've known the psycho and freak would become a couple. You know, birds of a feather and all that shit."

Her words hurt because she's insulting Colton, but I still can't think of a way to respond.

Then Colton steps between us and glares at her, "Jealous much?"

Feeling a little braver, I mutter, "Green isn't your color."

Colton lets out a burst of laughter, and throwing his arm around my shoulders, he nudges me forward. Glancing over his shoulder at Lindy, Colton says, "Stop looking for attention from Brie. It makes you look desperate."

Once we're a distance away from Lindy, Colton smiles down at me. "You did good."

I turn my gaze to him. "I did?"

"Yeah," he gives me a sideways hug.

It makes me feel ten feet tall, knowing Colton is happy with the single sentence I managed to get out.

Walking to class, my chin lifts slightly higher, and I don't feel as intimidated by the other students.

COLTON

When we get home, I go look for Mom while Brie changes out of her uniform.

"No, Jonah," I hear Mom say before I nudge her bedroom door open. Mom's pacing up and down at the foot of her bed, a frown on her face.

My heart immediately begins to beat faster, knowing she's talking to my father.

"I want a divorce." Mom lets out a huff and stops pacing, then hisses, "I won't let you near Colton." There's a couple of seconds pause from her, then her voice climbs with anger, "I don't care!"

I've never heard her talk that way to my father, and it fills me with hope that she's finally done with him.

"Don't come here," she bites the words out.

I move forward, and only when I reach for the phone does Mom notice me. She begins to pull away until I say, "Let me talk to him."

Mom hesitates for a moment, then relents and hands the device to me.

When I press it to my ear, I hear Dad say, "We all need to sit down and talk about this. I have to tie up things at the office, and then I'll fly out to Black Mountain."

"No, you won't," I growl, my anger quickly raging out of control just from hearing his voice.

"Colton?" Dad asks, and I can hear he's caught off guard. "Son?"

"I'm not your son," I grind through the rage, overwhelming me. "Don't you dare come here."

My eyes lock on Mom. She's gotten so much better the past few days. I don't want him near her.

Or Brie.

God, he'll undo everything.

"I have a right to see my family," he snaps.

"No, you don't. You lost that right a long time ago." My voice starts to tremble from all the effort it's taking to stay in control and not lose my shit. "I swear I'll put you in the ICU if you so much as set foot in this town. I won't hold back anymore."

"Oh, that's rich," he chuckles bitterly. "Fine, then I don't see why I have to pay for your sorry ass to attend that elite school. I'll cut off all financial aid to you and your mother."

My temper shoots through the ceiling, and I shout, "I've never wanted your money."

Mom grabs the phone from me and presses it to her ear. "Don't threaten Colton with money. You will pay alimony. My lawyer will be in touch." She cuts the call and then reaches for me. Wrapping me in a hug, she says, "He'll be out of our lives soon."

I shake my head and pull back. "Not as long as we're taking his money."

"It's his responsibility to pay alimony. Let me handle it."

I stare at Mom, and it's on the tip of my tongue to ask her if she really can handle it.

She must see the doubt on my face because she says, "I know I've let you down in the past, but I'll make up for it. I promise. I don't want you worrying about things anymore. I want you to focus on completing your senior year so you can go to college."

I shake my head hard. "I'll get a job. I'll look after us."

Mom lifts her hand and places it against my cheek. "My sweet boy. You've grown up too quickly." She shakes her head. "It's not your responsibility. I know you don't have much faith in me, but I... give me a chance to be the mother I never was."

I don't want to hurt her, but can't stop myself from asking, "Why now? Is it because of Brie?"

Mom's eyes lock on mine. "I'm not going to lie to you. Seeing what happened to Brie was a wake-up call. It was hard to accept what was happening to us, but Brie's circumstances have shined a bright light on it." Mom's voice begins to falter, and a tear sneaks over her cheek. "I let him abuse you. It's one hundred percent my fault. I should've protected you and Brady. I'll never forgive myself for allowing it to happen."

Emotion wells in my chest, and I clench my jaw.

Mom lets out a sob, then squeezes the words out, "I'm sorry, Colton. I'll always regret it, but I hope I can make it up to you."

What about Brady?

How will she make it up to him?

Part of me wants to hug Mom and tell her I forgive her for never protecting us. But, the other half of me is still too angry. Still too raw from losing my brother to such senseless violence.

'He abused her as well,' my heart whispers.

Torn in two, I can only shake my head.

I've been strong the past four months because I was scared I'd lose her as well. Now that she's getting better, the cracks are starting to show, and all the heartache is spilling back into my life.

"Please, don't hate me," she sobs.

I hate seeing her so upset, and again, I put my mom's needs before my own, and I pull her into a hug, murmuring, "I don't hate you. I just need time."

Mom nods. When we pull back, she says, "I promise to make it up to you."

Still, I don't want her dealing with my father alone, and it has me saying, "Don't make any decisions regarding us without talking to me first."

Mom nods. "Of course."

Feeling drained, I start to walk out of Mom's room, saying, "I'm going to change. I'm taking Brie out so she can show me the town. I think it would do her good."

"Maybe go see a movie," she offers an idea.

"If Brie wants to." I go straight to my room, and shutting the door, I stand and stare at the gray bedspread.

I've had to be the strong one for so long, and it's become hard to trust anyone. I don't think I'll ever be able to allow someone control over my life.

Mom wants to make up for where she failed us, but I know from experience that she's no match for my father. I need to get him out of our lives.

Chapter 17

BRIE

I've just changed into a pair of shorts and a t-shirt when Colton suddenly shouts, "I've never wanted your money."

My heartbeat begins to speed up, and I dart to the door. Peeking into the hallway, I can hear Colton and Mrs. Lawson talking, and it sounds like she's crying.

Crap. That can't be good.

What do I do?

"Why now? Is it because of Brie?" I hear Colton ask.

Am I the reason they're fighting? Is it because I moved in here?

I can't hear Mrs. Lawson's reply, and it makes me anxious. I don't want to be the reason for them fighting.

My hands begin to tremble, and I clasp them tightly together. I take a step backward as my anxiety spikes.

Minutes later, I hear Colton say, "I'm going to change. I'm taking Brie out so she can show me the town. I think it would do her good."

"Maybe go see a movie," Mrs. Lawson replies.

"If Brie wants to."

When Colton comes out of his mom's room, I dart deeper into my room, so he doesn't catch me eavesdropping and nervously gnaw at my bottom lip.

Shoot, what do I do now?

Uncertainty fills me, but I know I can't hide like a coward. My eyes anxiously dart around the room, and a sinking feeling inside me makes it feel as if my stomach is being sucked into a pit.

I need to find out if it's because of me. As much as I don't want to, I'd rather go back to my mother than cause Colton and Mrs. Lawson problems.

It's the right thing to do, but...

I don't want to go back to my mother.

Feeling at a total loss, my mind races for a solution.

Maybe I can... crap, I don't know.

Hopefully, I can find a job soon, and I'll only have to live with my mother until I've saved enough to afford my own place?

I inch closer to the hallway and glance at Mrs. Lawson's closed door, then I turn my gaze to Colton's. Quietly, I creep closer to Colton's room. I bring up my hand but hesitate.

I don't want them fighting because of me.

I bite my bottom lip again, and gathering up the courage, I knock on Colton's door.

"Yeah?"

I nudge the door open and see Colton lying on his bed with his legs draped over the side.

"Ah..." I begin, but the words dry up in my throat.

I really don't want to leave.

Colton glances at me, then sits up and mutters, "Oh, hey. Are you ready? Give me a second, and I'll change out of my school clothes."

Colton gets up from his bed and walks toward his closet. I shake my head, still clutching the doorknob.

I also can't stay if it's causing problems. I can't do that to them after they've been so kind to me.

"I... I didn't mean to, but I overheard... the fight," I stammer.

Colton lets out a sigh and shakes his head. "Sorry about that." He lifts his eyes to where I am, and they look tired.

I don't want to hurt him in any way, and it gives me the strength to say, "I don't want to cause you any trouble. I'll move out."

A frown instantly forms on his face. "What?" He walks to where I'm still standing by the door. "Why would you say that?"

"I... overheard," I mutter. "You asked your mom if it's because of me. I didn't hear the rest, but I... I don't want to disrupt your lives."

Colton lifts his hand and rubs the spot between his eyes. "It wasn't about you." He lets out another tired sigh. "My father called. He's being a dick."

Oh.

That changes things.

I'm relieved, and now that I don't have to worry about moving out today, I see the ache in Colton's eyes. "I'm sorry," I whisper as I push the door fully open. Closing the distance between us, I wrap my arms around his waist, and I hug him as tightly as I can.

A heartbeat passes before Colton hugs me back. He lowers his head, burying his face in my neck. We stand like that for the longest time before I pull a little back. Catching Colton's eyes, I ask, "Do you want to talk about it?"

I might not be able to help, but I can be there for him.

Colton turns away from me and walks to his closet. "It's okay. I'll just change quickly, then we can leave."

I stare at his back, and not knowing what else to do, I let out a sigh and walk back to my room.

Minutes later, Colton taps on my door. "Let's go." There's still a stormy look in his eyes, and again I wish I could make him feel better.

Feeling uncomfortable, I say, "We don't have to go out."

Colton forces a smile to his face, and it doesn't reach his eyes. "Come on. Getting out will do us both a world of good."

"Okay." I follow him out of the house, a frustrated sigh drifting over my lips. Colton always manages to cheer me up, and I have an overwhelming need to do the same for him.

But I don't know how to make him feel better.

We climb in the truck, and once we're driving down the street, Colton asks, "What are you showing me first?"

I think of all the places I can take him to, and knowing all the kids from school will be at Devil's Bluff, I shelf that idea. "Ah…" My mind races, and not able to come up with anything, I ask, "Do you want to walk around town? You can see all the stores?" Knowing I need to tell Colton about my looking for a job, I add, "I've been thinking about getting an after-school job. If we go to town, I'll be able to see if there are any vacancies."

A frown forms on Colton's face as he steers us in the direction of the main road. "Why do you want to get a job? It will interfere with your study time."

I shrug, and glancing out of the window at the houses passing by, I awkwardly mutter, "I need to get some form of income. I can't just live off you and your mom."

And what if something goes wrong and I have to leave?

COLTON

I know it's only normal for Brie to think of finances, but it's the last thing I want her worrying about.

I glance at Brie and see that she's staring out of the window. She's clutching her hands together, and it's clear she's tense.

I place my right hand over hers and give it a squeeze before putting it back on the wheel. "You trust me, right?"

Brie nods, turning her eyes to me. "Yeah."

"It's our senior year, Brie, and if you want to go to college, you'll have to study hard. It will add a ton of pressure if you get a job on top of all the school work."

Pressure she doesn't need right now.

"I know," she mutters. She lets out a sigh, then explains, "It's just... what if we get in a fight or I do something to upset your mom? Where would I go then?"

There's a public park on our left, and I pull the truck over to the curb. Turning off the engine, I push my door open as I say, "Let's go to the park."

Climbing out, I wait for Brie and then start to walk. I spot a bench under a tree and head in that direction. Reaching it, I ask, "Want to sit?"

"Sure."

I take a seat, and leaning forward, I rest my forearms on my thighs before addressing Brie's worry. "I understand your concern, Brie. I'd be worried as well if I were in your position. All I can say is we won't kick you out on the street."

Brie also leans forward, and she tightly clasps her hands while staring at the ground. "You can't say that for sure. What if something goes wrong?"

Keeping in mind that all the fights Brie had to face were never in her favor, I reply, "Let's say we get into a fight, I'm not going to demand you leave. We'll talk about whatever caused the argument and deal with it. Like normal people do." I turn my eyes to her. "I'm not a petty person, Brie. I'll never do that to you. The day I brought you home, I took responsibility for you."

Brie shakes her head, a miserable look tightening her features. "I know you're a good person, but... I shouldn't be your responsibility. You're only a year older than me. You have your own life to worry about."

Brie needs to feel like she's contributing to the household, or she'll never feel like she's a part of it. I change my strategy and say, "Let me put it another way then. Up until you moved in, I was doing everything around the house." I suck in a breath of air and admit, "My mom hardly left her room."

Brie brings her eyes up to mine. "Gosh, I didn't know. I'm sorry. That must've been tough."

"Yeah, but now you're living with us. You can help me, and honestly, my mom's been much better with you around." I turn toward Brie and place my hand over hers. "Brie, you're helping us as much as we're helping you." I can see my words are starting to get through to her, and a smile begins to play around my mouth. "I promise we'll never kick you out." I scrunch my nose, knowing that never is a long time, then add, "Unless you do something terrible, like kill someone." I let out a chuckle. "And that also depends on who you kill. I'm willing to help get rid of *specific* bodies."

Brie lets out a burst of laughter. "Don't worry. I can't even bring myself to kill an ant."

Our eyes meet, and I murmur, "I wouldn't have invited you to stay if I wasn't serious about it. I want you to feel at home. Don't worry about finances."

"Living with my mother, money was the one thing I've never had to worry about," Brie admits. "I've always had everything I needed because my mother didn't want people talking. Also, my grandparents kept giving her money so she would stay here and not move back to California." She takes a deep breath. "It's funny how much can change in the space of a couple of days."

"Yeah," I agree. Giving her hand another squeeze, I ask, "Do you feel better now?"

She nods, then asks, "So you'll let me help around the house? I can do the laundry and keep the house clean. I can —"

I let out a chuckle and stand up, interrupting Brie's rambling, "I get a feeling if I don't stop you, you'll do everything. We'll split the chores. Okay?"

Brie gets up and nods, a smile stretching over her face. "I'd like that."

I glance around the park, then say, "Well, we've kind of seen the park. Where are we going next?"

Brie draws her bottom lip between her teeth while she thinks, then asks, "Have you been to Anderson's bookstore?"

I shake my head.

"You're missing out then. They have the best art supplies in town. Oh, and books, of course."

Walking back to the truck, I interlink my fingers with Brie's, feeling much better now that we got that problem out of the way.

"Colton," she murmurs next to me.

"Yeah."

Brie brings her other hand to the inside of my elbow and pressing her cheek to my shoulder, she whispers, "It's nice having someone I can talk to."

We reach the truck, and I open the passenger door for her with a broad smile on my face.

The drive is quick to the bookstore, and when we walk inside, Brie gestures toward the aisles of books. "That's the fiction side, and over there, you'll find all the other categories." Then she points to our right. "That's my section."

I pull Brie toward the sketchpads and ask, "Do you need anything?"

She shakes her head. "I got what I needed before school started."

My gaze falls on a row of pretty pens and journals, and I walk toward it. "Have you ever journaled before?"

Brie shakes her head and picks up one with shades of soft pink and gold, and the words '*Unicorn Dreams*' scribbled on the front.

"You want that one?" I ask.

Brie shakes her head and puts it back.

One catches my eyes, and loving the words on the cover, I read, "Shit, I can't say out loud." We both chuckle, and then I say, "I'll get you this one."

"What for?" Brie asks.

"To write all the things you can't say out loud." I wrap my arm around her shoulder and steer her toward the biography section. "I'm looking for a specific book."

"Which one?" Brie asks as glances over the titles.

"Autobiography of a Yogi, by Paramahansa Yogananda." I suck at pronouncing the author's name and feeling awkward, I explain, "Apparently, it was the only ebook found on Steve Jobs' IPad."

We search through the books until Brie shakes her head. "Give me a second." I watch her walk over to the cashier, and after a couple of minutes, she comes back grinning. "They checked on the system, and they have one in stock. They'll find it for us. Come." She grabs my hand and pulls me back toward the cashier.

When they bring us the book, Brie looks happier than me. I give her a sideways hug. "Thanks, that saved a lot of time."

I pay for the two books with the credit card Mom gave me after we moved in so I could do all the shopping for us.

Leaving the store, I ask, "Where to now?"

Brie glances up and down the street. "The rest of the stores are all basic."

"Want to get something to drink?" I ask, pointing at the diner at the end of the street.

Brie shakes her head. "There will be kids from school."

"So?" I raise an eyebrow at her. "Don't let that stop you."

When I take a step in the direction of the diner, Brie grabs hold of my hand. "I really don't want to go there. We can get something from a drive-thru and go back to the park."

Not wanting to push her, I relent. "Okay."

We each get a milkshake before I drive back to the public park. Once we're seated on the bench, I take a sip, then gesture to the bag with our books. "You're going to use the journal, right?"

Brie nods, and setting her milkshake down on the side of the bench, she pulls my book out of the bag and begins to page through it.

She stops to read something, and it has me saying, "Read it out loud."

She clears her throat and shoots me a shy grin before she reads, "You may wander through the universe incognito. Make vessels of the gods. Be ever youthful. You may walk in water and live in fire. But control of the mind is better and more difficult."

She actually looks impressed with what she just read, and glancing up at me, she says, "I think I need to start reading the same books as you."

"Why?" I ask with a chuckle.

A look I haven't seen before settles on Brie's face, and it makes my heartbeat speed up. "Because you're the best person I know, Colton. I want to be more like you."

Lifting my hand, I brush her bangs away from where it's hanging in her eye. "You're pretty special just as you are, Brie."

Her lips curve up as a soft pink blush blossoms on her cheeks.

Chapter 18

BRIE

I follow Colton to the laundry room on Saturday morning. We've decided to get all the chores done.

I have to admit, this is the first time I'm excited about doing any kind of housework. If I can do my part, then I'll feel better about living here.

"Let's separate the whites from the colors," Colton says.

I grab my basket, and I dig all my school shirts out of it. Then my eyes fall on the white bra, and my eyebrows shoot up.

Dang.

I glance at Colton while heat spreads up my neck. I obviously didn't think this through.

Colton notices I've stopped and glances at me. "What's wrong?"

"Ah…" The blush on my face deepens, and I quickly lower my eyes only to stare at the bra again, mumbling, "This is so awkward."

"What?" He begins to move closer, and I quickly cover the bra.

"Uh…" I let out a breath, then push through and ask, "How are we going to do the underwear?"

Colton instantly bursts out laughing and shaking his head, he goes back to sorting the clothes while saying, "Brie, I've seen women's underwear before."

Yeah, but they weren't mine.

I stand and stare at Colton until he says, "Okay, separate yours. I'll do my mother's and mine later."

I shake my head. "It will be a waste of water and soap to wash mine separately." Shrugging, I add, "Don't mind me. I'm just being silly."

I add my whites to Colton's pile and sucking it up, I pull the bra out of the laundry basket and quickly tuck it under a shirt.

"You're cute," Colton murmurs, a huge grin on his face.

When the bundle of whites is in the washing machine, we head downstairs. Colton vacuums and dusts the living room while I take care of the kitchen.

225

Before we know it, we're all done inside.

"Now for outside," Colton says.

I frown at him. "Do you always do everything on Saturdays?"

He shakes his head. "No, but now that you're here, I'd rather get everything done. That way, we don't have to worry about it during the week."

I follow Colton outside, and he points to the flower beds. "You can start pulling the weeds while I mow the lawn."

"Okay."

"Get a trash bag from the pantry."

"Okay." I dart back inside, and just as I grab a bag, Mrs. Lawson walks into the kitchen.

"You and Colton are working so hard I thought I'd make some sandwiches."

I nod and begin to inch my way out of the kitchen.

"Brie," Mrs. Lawson says, and I instantly stop moving. A smile wavers around her lips. "I know you have to get used to me, but I want you to know I'll never treat you the way your mother did."

It feels like someone just launched a rocket filled with emotions through me. My eyes begin to blur, and I blink fast in an attempt to keep the tears back. Finally, I manage to nod.

"I know it will take time," Mrs. Lawson continues. "But I'm here if you need anything."

"Thank you, Mrs. Lawson." My voice sounds hoarse to my own ears, and I clear my throat.

"Please call me Cassie," she says, her smile a little wider.

"Okay."

"I'll call you and Colton once lunch is ready."

I nod again before I dart out of the kitchen. Once I'm outside, I suck in a deep breath of air while trying to regain control over my emotions.

Mostly I feel... sadish? I think it's because I don't want to be weird around Cassie, but I just can't help it.

I begin to pull the weeds while my thoughts run circles around Cassie. I really need to try harder with her. So far, she's done nothing to hurt me.

My eyes dart to Colton as he comes around the house, and then I can only stare. *Holy crap.* He has a baseball cap on backward, and it makes him look hot.

He catches me staring and asks, "You okay?"

I quickly nod and snap my eyes back to the flowerbed. "Yeah."

While Colton mows the lawn, I keep stealing glances, and each one has my heart beating faster.

Colton then goes to the backyard while I'm stuck in front, and I can't help but pout.

When I'm done pulling all the weeds out, I carry the bag to the back, and as I round the corner of the house, I come to a sudden stop.

Colton's coming out of the shed and grabbing hold of the back of his shirt, he pulls it over his head.

My eyebrows pop up, and my mouth drops open when I see his abs.

Wow.

Just wow.

There's a fluttering in my stomach, and as he walks toward me, I can't deny the fact that I have feelings for Colton.

Shoot. Trust me to develop a crush on my best friend.

When his eyes settle on me, I become nervous, and not wanting him to find out how I feel about him, I carry the bag over to the trashcan before darting into the house.

———————

COLTON

Something's wrong.

I watch as Brie focuses on her sandwich.

"Are you sure you're okay?" I ask again.

She keeps her eyes on her plate. "Uh-huh."

Yep, something is definitely wrong.

"Did something happen?" I ask, determined to get to the bottom of whatever's bothering her.

She shakes her head, eyes still glued to the plate. "No."

Placing my elbows on the table, I lean forward and tilt my head. "Brie."

She sets her half-eaten sandwich down and takes a sip of water before she finally looks at me. "I promise. Nothing's wrong."

I keep staring at her until a blush stains her neck and cheeks.

Brie gets up and takes our plates to the sink, then asks, "Is there anything else we still have to do?"

Walking into the kitchen, Mom says, "I've taken care of the laundry. I've set your clothes on your bed, Brie." She glances between Brie and me. "What are your plans for the rest of the afternoon?"

"Do you want to go out?" I ask Brie.

She shrugs. "Or we can just stay at home and watch a movie."

"I can make some popcorn," Mom offers. "But, I suppose you both want to get cleaned up first."

"Definitely," Brie says before she darts out of the kitchen, and all I can do is sit here and frown. She was normal with Mom.

Did I do something?

"What's wrong?" Mom asks. She comes to take a seat at the table.

I shake my head. "It's probably my imagination."

A smile forms around Mom's lips. "You like her, don't you?"

My eyes latch onto my mother's, and it takes a couple of seconds before I admit, "Yeah, I do."

"Just take it slow. Okay?" Mom warns. "Brie's been through a lot."

"I know." I sit back in my chair. "Trust me, I know."

There's a flash of guilt on Mom's face. "I'm sorry."

I shake my head, not wanting her to think I was referring to my father abusing us. "I mean, I know Brie needs time. Chances are we'll just remain friends. It's probably better that way."

Mom shakes her head. "Once Brie is settled and things are better, I don't see why you can't date each other. That's if she feels the same way about you. Most relationships start out as friendship. All I'm saying is take it slow, and once things get serious, use protection."

"Mom!" I get up and start to walk away. "I already learned everything in health class. We don't have to have that conversation."

Mom's laughter follows me as I dart up the stairs. I'm just about to walk into my bedroom when the bathroom door opens, and Brie darts out.

The second she sees me, she points inside. "There's a spider in the tub."

I let out a chuckle. "I'll take care of it."

I roll some toilet paper off, but then Brie says, "Don't kill it."

"I won't." I move closer to the bathtub with Brie hovering close behind me. Opening the window first, I then patiently wait for the spider to climb onto the toilet paper before letting the paper hang out of the window. The spider finally climbs off and scurries away. "All done. It's safe to bathe," I tease Brie.

She grins happily, and it makes me think it was all my imagination thinking there was something wrong.

After I'm done showering, and I'm dressed in a comfortable pair of sweatpants and a t-shirt, I walk to the living room.

The house smells like popcorn, and there's a massive bowl on the coffee table, along with a bowl of M&M's and three glasses of coke.

Brie's sitting on the one couch, and Mom's on the other, so I plop down next to Brie, who's scrolling through the list of movies on Netflix. Her eyes are wide, and she's holding her bottom lip captive between her teeth.

"There are so many," she mutters. "Which one should we watch?"

"I think you'll like this one." I take the remote from Brie and scroll *To All The Boys I've Loved Before,* then press play. "It was pretty popular when it came out."

"Yay, a romance," Mom cheers. She grabs a handful of popcorn and wiggles her butt into a comfortable position. "I love this one."

"You know they made a sequel, right?" I say as I take some M&M's.

"We can watch it after this one." Mom looks more excited than us, and it makes a smile spread over my face.

Brie keeps sitting on the edge of the couch, and every now and then, she takes one popcorn. Her eyes are glued to the screen, and as the minutes tick by, the smile on her face grows.

We're already twenty minutes into the movie when I realize I'm still staring at Brie, watching her reaction instead of the TV.

It's freaking amazing.

She lets out a chuckle when something funny happens, and her lips part when there's an intense scene. But then there's a sad moment, and she pouts.

Holy shit.

I'll never be able to say no to her if she gives me that look.

This girl is cute and beautiful, and… off the charts hot.

She's nothing short of perfect.

And it's safe to say I'm hopelessly crushing on her.

When Brie's had enough popcorn, she scoots back. Knowing Mom won't mind, I place my arm around Brie's shoulders, and I pull her closer. When Brie leans into me, a contented smile sticks to my face throughout the remainder of the movie.

When it's finished, we take a restroom break before we start the next movie. The intro is still playing when Mom says, "After this, we can watch The Kissing Booth."

I let out a chuckle. "Only if you make us mac and cheese."

"Deal."

The atmosphere is relaxing, and we're all smiling.

"This is nice," Mom whispers.

"Yeah," I agree.

Brie's smile widens, and then she says, "I love it. I've always wanted to do this."

I pull her back against my side and press a kiss to her hair.

"We should make Saturday's movie nights from now on," I mention.

"That's a good idea," Mom agrees.

With my arm around Brie, I begin to brush my thumb softly over the skin above her elbow while we watch the movie.

Chapter 19

BRIE

It's been two weeks since I moved in with the Lawsons, and after that one message from my mother, I haven't heard from her again.

Sometimes I feel guilty for just leaving her the way I did, but then I remind myself she's abusive and mean. She's never showed me any kind of love, and it's okay that I don't miss her.

I feel I'm more comfortable with Cassie now that some time has passed. Living in a calm environment has helped a lot. I had another flashback when a glass accidentally slipped from my hands while I was washing it. Luckily it didn't break, and Colton was there to calm me down. I wrote about it in the journal Colton gave me, focusing on how I felt after it happened. At least, I wasn't consumed with shame like the time before, and I'm taking it as a win.

Things at school are better as well. Michael has moved on to looking for trouble with a new girl in school, Monica

Romero. He got on Cole Travis' wrong side because of it, and it seems like he'll be kicked out of the band. I couldn't care less.

Sully, on the other hand, still pops up every now and then, but every time he tries to bully me, Colton is there to get rid of him.

Lindy's still… just Lindy. She'll make nasty comments to which Colton always has a response. I know I can't let him keep fighting my battles, but it's hard to think of a comeback in the heat of the moment.

Walking into my art class, I take my seat and open my sketchpad. I'm working on a picture of Colton and what he looked like on the first day of school. Now that I know him better, I understand why he seemed so angry. He hasn't spoken much of his brother, Brady, and I'm worried he's bottling up all his heartache. He's always so focused on me and solving my problems, and I worry it's not giving him any time to deal with his own past.

I've been trying to think of a way to help him, but I'm at a total loss.

Miss Snow goes to stand in front of the class. "There's an art competition hosted by the University of Black Mountain. The winner will win five thousand dollars toward their financial aid should they choose to attend an art course there. I'm hoping you'll all enter."

All my attention is on Miss Snow because it would help a lot if I could win that money.

"You can use any medium. You can create anything. The deadline is in two weeks. I have entry forms, so come see me if you're interested in taking part."

One of the girls raises her hand and asks, "Can we work on it during class?"

Miss Snow nods. "You can. To be fair to those who aren't entering the competition, I'll have this project count toward your yearly mark."

Oh wow. What am I going to draw?

My mind races with so many ideas but none of them stick.

"If you need some ideas, I have a couple," Miss Snow says, and my eyes dart to her. "You can create something to express a current issue, like global warming or deforestation. Or make something that represents your life or how you feel. As long as you're passionate about it."

Honestly, the only thing I'm passionate about is Colton.

I pull an awkward face as I look down at the image of him I'm working on. For now, I carry on with it, needing to complete it before I start with the new project.

I manage to finish the sketch minutes before the bell rings, and gathering my stuff, I walk up to Miss Snow's desk. "Can I have an entry form, please?"

"Sure. I'm glad you're taking part. When you have your work ready, bring it to me with the completed form."

A smile tugs at my lips as I take the paper from her. With my thoughts on what I can work on, I make my way to my history class.

An arm falls around my shoulders, and for a moment, I think it's Colton, but when I look up, I see that it's Sully. He grips me tightly. "Where's your bodyguard?"

I try to shrug his arm off, but he only tightens his hold, letting out a taunting chuckle. "You know, I thought you were a lesbian, Weinstock, but seeing as Lawson's always hanging onto you, I must've been wrong."

Instead of the usual fear that makes me cower back, anger begins to bubble in my chest, and I try to pull my shoulders free again. Sully doesn't let go and uses his body to push me up against the wall. When he starts to lower his head, and his lips are inches from mine, my heart almost explodes from my chest.

There's no way he's going to be my first kiss!

Bringing both my hands up between us, I push Sully so hard that I actually manage to shove him away from me.

"Don't…" I gulp hard, but then my anger wins over the fear, and I snap, "Don't touch me." Darting away from him, I even manage to mutter, "Asshole."

I stalk into history, still upset that Sully actually tried to kiss me. Slamming my sketchpad down on the desk, I plop down in the chair and scowl.

I just wish Sully would get the damn message and leave me be.

A hand on my shoulder has me instantly yanking away and glaring up at whoever's bothering me now. When I see Colton, I let out a sigh and slump back in my chair.

The frown on his face has me explaining, "Sorry, I thought you were someone else."

"Like who?" he asks, sitting down at his own desk.

"Stupid Sully," I grumble. "He just tried to kiss me."

"What?" A deadly look spreads over Colton's face, darkening his eyes until they're almost black.

When he glances around the class for Sully, and he begins to get up, I reach over to him and grab hold of his arm. "Don't. You'll get in trouble with Mr. Donati. Besides, I pushed him away and told him not to touch me."

Colton's eyebrows pop up, and a smile forms around his face. "You did?"

I nod, and now that I'm feeling calmer, it's starting to sink in that I actually stood up for myself. "Yeah..." I murmur, because it feels a little surreal, "I did."

"That's my girl," Colton brags, looking impressed with me. "I knew you had it in you."

Mr. Donati begins with class, and it's hard to pay attention because I'm too caught up in how good it feels that Colton is proud of me.

———————

After school, we stop at the store to get paint. With it being my birthday tomorrow, Colton said we should get the painting done tonight, then we don't have to do it on my birthday.

When we get home, we change out of our school uniforms and then push the bed away from the wall. Colton spreads a plastic tarp over the carpet while I position the two ladders on opposite sides so we can each paint one half.

For a while, we work in silence, then Colton chuckles. "Blue is definitely your color."

I glance at the parts we've painted. "Yeah, the baby blue looks good."

"You have paint on your face," he says, pointing to his own cheek.

"Oh." I wipe over my left cheek, and it makes him laugh.

"No, you're making it worse." Colton walks over to me, and taking the roller from me, he sets it on the tarp. Then he takes hold of my hand and pulls me to the bathroom.

Glancing in the mirror, a smile pulls at my lips. I have a couple of streaks over my face. I check my hands, and seeing the blotches of blue, I let out a chuckle.

Colton wets a cloth, then comes to stand in front of me. He brings his other hand to my chin, and he wipes at the smudges.

After a couple of seconds, he whispers, "So you told Sully to leave you alone?"

"Yeah." I glance up at him and admit, "At first I was scared, but then I got angry. There was no way I was going to let him kiss me." I shrug. "Plus, you've shown me how to deal with him. I can't let you keep fighting my battles."

"I don't mind." His voice is a low murmur.

A spine-tingling sensation ripples over me, and I'm unable to drop my eyes from his gaze.

Colton's movements slow, and my heart begins to beat rapidly as he starts to lean down. My breaths grow faster as anticipation builds between us.

Oh, gosh.

I'm too scared to move, not wanting to disturb the moment between us.

"Guys," Cassie suddenly calls from the hallway.

We instantly pull apart, and Colton darts to the sink to rinse the cloth while I almost step into the shower.

"Do you want anything to drink?" There's a moment's pause, then Cassie calls, "Colton. Where are you?"

"In here," he replies. His voice sounds hoarse, and he quickly clears his throat.

Appearing in the doorway, Cassie says, "Oh, there you are."

My eyes dart to her while my heart is still thumping hard in my chest from what almost happened between Colton and me. I hope she can't see any of my emotions on my face.

Cassie notices the paint on my face and lets out a chuckle. "It's going to take more than water to get that paint off your face."

Oh, right. The paint.

COLTON

I drape the cloth over the side of the bath, then say, "I'll pour us some coke." I squeeze past Brie and my mom, then add, "Mom, will you help Brie get the paint off?"

"Sure."

Darting out of the bathroom, I rush down the hallway and take the stairs two at a time. Only when I'm in the kitchen, do I stop. I place my hands on the counter, and staring at the granite top, I suck in a deep breath of air.

What was I thinking? I almost kissed Brie.

Mom almost caught us. Not that she would mind, but still, I don't want our first kiss to happen next to a damn toilet where my mom can walk in on us. And I definitely don't want it happening on the same day that idiot tried to kiss Brie.

I shake my head and move to grab two glasses from the cupboard. I pour the coke, and only when I place the bottle back in the fridge do I realize Brie didn't pull away.

Did she want me to kiss her?

It doesn't escape my attention that Brie stood up to Sully for the first time today because he tried to kiss her, but she didn't push me away.

The corners of my mouth begin to lift at the thought.

Does that mean she wants me to kiss her?

It's only been two weeks, though. Yeah, Brie is doing much better, and she's even more relaxed with my mother. But isn't it too soon?

Picking up the glasses, I carry them back upstairs while I mull over all the questions in my head. I find the women in Brie's room, and I hand her the soda.

"Do you want to get a blue bedspread?" Mom asks Brie.

Brie first swallows the sip she just took, then answers, "Yeah, or it can be gray like Colton's."

Mom glances around the room. "We need to get you a dresser and a table and chair."

Brie smiles at Mom. "That will be great. Thank you."

"We'll go after school tomorrow." Mom begins to walk toward the door. "I'm going to start with dinner while you guys finish up in here."

Mom leaves the room, and Brie's eyes dart to me before they snap to the wall.

Should we talk about what almost happened between us?

Ah… Nope, not yet.

I set the glass down and grab the roller. Clearing my throat, I say, "At least my mom got the paint off your face."

"Yeah," Brie mutters as she dips her roller in the paint.

The silence that falls between us feels both awkward and electrifying.

I wonder how Brie feels about me. Damn, if she's not attracted to me, I'm screwed. I really don't want to be the best friend that doesn't get the girl. That would suck a hell of a lot.

Chapter 20

BRIE

When I wake up with Colton's chest rising under my cheek, a broad smile spreads over my face.

We slept on the couch because my room smells like paint, and Colton wouldn't hear about me sleeping in my bed.

It's my birthday. I'm eighteen!

The thought broadens my smile.

Careful not to wake Colton, I climb over him and off the couch. Wanting to do something nice for them, I take some bacon and eggs from the fridge. It's basically the only thing I can make without setting fire to the kitchen.

Grinning, I first fry the bacon. While I break the eggs into a bowl, I start to softly hum a tune. I beat them until they look fluffy enough while my thoughts turn to 'the almost' kiss. At least, I think that's what it was. Colton hasn't said anything about it, and I'm not about to bring it up.

I glance at the living room and grin when I see Colton leaning against the back of the couch, his arms crossed over his chest as he watches me with a smile on his face.

"Morning," I chirp happily.

"Morning." Pushing away from the couch, he walks toward me. He stops really close to me, and my stomach flutters as he brings his hands up, framing my face. "Happy Birthday." Then he leans down, and my heart stops as his lips brush over my cheek.

I struggle to breathe and can only blink when he pulls back.

Wow. If it was that intense just from Colton kissing my cheek, I wonder what an actual kiss will feel like.

Probably like fireworks going off.

"Are you making breakfast?" Colton's voice sounds hoarse, and he clears his throat.

I take a deep breath, and scrunching my nose, I turn back to the stove to pour some of the eggs into the pan. "I wanted to do something nice. I can't promise it will be as good as your mom's, though."

Colton steals a piece of bacon, and I watch as he eats it. When he doesn't comment on how it tastes, I lift an eyebrow at him. "And?"

A grin that's nothing short of heart-stopping pulls at his mouth. "It's good." I keep staring at him until he points at the stove. "The eggs are going to burn."

"Shoot!" I quickly stir them while a blush creeps up my neck.

Colton begins to set the table, and I'm super aware of how he moves around the kitchen.

I really like Colton, and it's not just because he's helped me so much. It's because he has the kindest heart, the bravest soul, and a smile... that makes my heart beat faster in a way it never has before.

This life might not have been easy so far, but Colton's light has a way of breaking through the dark.

The corner of my mouth curves up.

I'm in love for the first time.

"I think the eggs are done," Colton says, snapping me out of my thoughts.

Focusing on what I'm doing, I see that they're a minute away from burning and quickly scoop them out into a plate.

Dang, that was close.

"Morning," Cassie says as she walks into the kitchen. "Are you guys making breakfast?"

Colton shakes his head. "Brie is. I'll make coffee."

Cassie comes to me, and when she wraps her arm around my shoulder and gives me a sideways hug, I don't feel as anxious as I used to.

"Happy Birthday, sweetheart," she says before pressing a kiss to my cheek.

This time I have a different reaction from when Colton kissed me. My eyes dart to Cassie's, and seeing the warmth on her face makes me feel emotional.

Between falling in love and experiencing a mother's love for the first time, it makes tears threaten.

I quickly blink them away and focus on the eggs while rambling, "Bacon and eggs are the only two things I can make. I hope you don't mind."

"I'm sure it will taste great," Cassie encourages me before she goes to sit by the table.

When I'm done, I place the bacon and eggs on the table. Taking a breath, I gather the guts to ask, "Cassie, when you're not busy, can you teach me how to cook?"

A smile instantly widens around her mouth. "Of course. You should stand with me when I make dinner. That way, you'll learn faster."

Colton brings our coffee, and we sit down.

"That will be great," I reply.

I wait for Colton and Cassie to grab some bacon and eggs first, and then I add some to my plate.

I watch Cassie take a bite of the eggs and anxiously wait to see if she likes it. She gives me a reassuring smile. "It's delicious."

Feeling happy, I dig into my own breakfast.

Shopping with Colton and Cassie is surreal. They're just as excited as me and keep pulling me from one item to the next.

We settled on a gray bedspread and matching pillowcases.

I'm secretly happy because it looks like Colton's.

Cassie chose a beautiful white dressing table and matching stool while Colton found some fairy lights. He said he'll put them up around the mirror that comes with the dressing table.

Standing in the middle of the store, I glance around me. I notice all the families, and then my eyes turn back to Colton and Cassie, and for the first time, it feels like I'm part of something bigger. I'm no longer just surviving.

I belong.

I have a family.

Cassie's eyes land on a huge dreamcatcher, and she points at it excitedly while shouting, "Brie, what do you think of this for your wall?"

I let out a burst of laughter and walk over to where she is. "It's pretty." The dreamcatcher looks like it's been crocheted with ribbons hanging from it.

"Do you want it?" Cassie asks.

I glance at her and feeling that they've gotten me so much already, I say, "Maybe another time. You've already bought me so much."

Cassie begins to pout, and my eyes grow huge. Then she actually whines, "But there's still a whole bunch of things I wanted to get." She pulls a cute face, and I begin to chuckle. "Please."

"How can I say no now?" I laugh.

"So we're taking the dreamcatcher?" she asks, excitement all over her face.

"Yeah."

I help Cassie put the dreamcatcher in a cart, and then we make our way over to where Colton is looking at floating shelves.

When he notices us, he says, "I can put a couple of these on the sides of the bed. You can use them for books or whatever you want."

I glance at Cassie, and she instantly bats her eyelashes at me, all cutely saying, "We should definitely get them."

Grinning at her, I shake my head, then mumble, "I can't say no when your mom pulls that face."

Colton lets out a chuckle. "Yeah? You should see how cute you look when you do that."

Huh?

"When did I pull a face like that?"

Colton's gaze snaps to me as if he just realized he said that to me, and then he begins to load shelves in the cart, mumbling, "While we were watching a movie." Then he walks away.

"Oh my gosh," Cassie exclaims, drawing my attention. "Brie, aren't those the same color blue as the wall?"

She's pointing at a throw and tiny pillows. I walk closer with her and run my fingers over the fabric. "It's so soft. They look the same color."

Cassie grabs a throw and says, "Take two pillows."

Knowing she'll get her way if I try to decline, I pick them up and carry them to the cart that's reaching its capacity.

I look at everything they've gotten me so far, and emotion wells in my chest because not once did they make me feel like a burden like my mother would've.

"Thank you so much," I say to Cassie before I close the distance between us and wrap my arms around her. "You're really the best mother ever."

Cassie hugs me back and presses a kiss to my cheek before we pull apart. Her eyes shine, and there's a wide smile on her face. "You're welcome, sweetheart. It makes me happy seeing you happy."

Colton and Cassie are making this birthday unforgettable, not because of the things they're buying me, but because of the way they're doing it. They make me feel special.

As long as I live, I'll never forget the past two weeks, even if the worst happens, and we go our separate ways. Cassie and Colton will always be the first people who loved me.

The first I loved.

COLTON

After we carry everything into the house, I go get my toolkit and get started on putting the shelves up.

I position the first one and glance over my shoulder at Brie. "Is it good here, or do you want it higher?"

She walks closer. "A little lower, or I won't be able to reach it."

My eyes dart between her and the wall, and then I mutter, "True." I glance at the other wall. "And you want the dreamcatcher on that wall, right?"

"Please." I grin at her happy face, and while I'm drilling holes in the wall, Brie goes to get the vacuum cleaner so she can clean the mess I'm making.

Mom comes into the room and says, "Brie, I'm going to wash your new bedding. Okay?"

"Let me help." Brie drops the vacuum cleaner and goes to help remove everything from the packaging before she comes back to continue cleaning.

When I'm done, and the dreamcatcher and all the shelves are up, I assemble the dressing table and stool. It's already past seven when I'm done.

I go wash my hands, and as I pass Brie's room, I say, "Come on. Time to make dinner."

"Huh?" She catches up to me as I walk down the hallway. "You know I can't cook."

"Yeah, that's why I'm giving you your first lesson tonight."

"Really?" A wide smile stretches over her face. "What are you going to make?"

"Nachos."

Brie's eyes shine with excitement as we walk into the kitchen. "Get the cheddar and Colby Jack cheese from the fridge."

I open the bag of tortilla chips and empty it on a baking tray. When Brie comes to stand next to me, I say, "I got these at the local store because they're fried-in-house. They're thicker and sturdier."

I keep explaining what I'm doing as I place the chips in the oven so they can pre-bake while I prepare the ground beef, beans, and jalapenos for toppings.

Once we're done, and the nachos are back in the oven so the cheese can melt, I grin at Brie. "How was your first cooking lesson."

"Information overload," the words pop from her. "I need to write it all down."

I let out a chuckle. "You'll get the hang of it."

"How did you learn to cook?" Brie asks.

My smile wavers. To keep busy, I pour us each a glass of coke while I say, "After we moved here, it was either I learn how to cook or live off fast food."

Her eyes dart up to mine, and a sad expression tightens her features. "I'm sorry you had to go through that. I'll learn how to cook quickly, so I can help with dinner."

She's so damn adorable. I want to squeeze her tightly, but instead, keep still and say, "You did great with breakfast this morning. I'm sure you'll learn fast."

A grin spreads over her face, and again I'm filled with the urge to hug the hell out of her.

Trying to keep my cool, I ask, "How's your birthday so far?"

Her grin widens, and a light of happiness makes her eyes shine so clear, I can only stare.

God, can I fall any deeper for her?

"It's amazing." She lets out an excited squeak and suddenly darts forward, throwing her arms around my neck. There's zero hesitation on my part, and I wrap her up in a tight hug, lifting her off her feet. Then she whispers, "Thank you so much." I feel her words in the deepest part of me.

"You're welcome," I murmur before setting her back on her feet.

Turning to the oven, I remove the nachos. "Let's eat."

Chapter 21

BRIE

~~Dear Diary~~

~~Hey~~

Dear me,

Happy birthday! You made it to eighteen.

Today was unforgettable. Not because of all the gifts I got, but because of Colton and Cassie. I'm so lucky to have met them.

And Colton. I'm so in love with him. My heart keeps beating out of my chest, and I get all sweaty. Whenever I'm near him, it feels like my stomach ~~is going to~~ will explode from all the flutters.

He's my first love. Even though I hope he'll return my feelings one day, I'll still love him if he doesn't.

Anyway, I just wanted to write down how I feel because I can't share it with him. Yet. Maybe one day.

B.

Every day I wake up and see the shelves and dreamcatcher Colton put up, I smile.

I never thought life could be so good.

Since my room was redecorated, I only get to sleep on the couch with Colton on Friday and Saturday nights. We usually watch a movie before talking until we fall asleep.

Where I used to dread weekends, I now live for them.

Unfortunately, it's only Thursday. After getting ready for school, I go down to the kitchen, where I find Cassie preparing oatmeal for us.

"Morning," I say, making my way over to the coffee pot. "Can I make you a cup?"

"Morning, sweetie." She smiles at me. "Yes, please."

With every day that passes, I become more comfortable with Cassie. Mostly when I tense up around her and panic begins to tighten my insides, I just take deep breaths and push through. It's getting easier, though.

I place a cup of coffee on the counter near Cassie and then sip on my own.

Colton comes into the kitchen just as Cassie scoops three bowls of oatmeal.

"Did you sleep well?" he asks while fixing himself a cup of coffee.

"Yeah, and you?"

He shoots me a grin. "Like a baby."

"Babies don't sleep," Cassie says with a chuckle.

Just as we're about to sit down to eat, my phone begins to ring. Frowning, I pull it out of my jacket's pocket, and not recognizing the number, I answer, "Brie speaking."

"Where the hell are you?" a man's voice snaps over the line.

Frowning, I glance at Colton and Cassie, who are both staring at me. "Excuse me? I think you have the wrong number."

"You're talking with Bill Weinstock," he practically growls.

It takes a couple of seconds for the name to sink in, and a gasp escapes my lips. It's my grandfather.

Why would he call me?

"Some daughter you are! Serena was found dead two days ago. Where the hell have you been? Your mother died falling down the stairs. I'm blaming…"

The rest of his words fade as the shocking realization ripples over me.

My mother's dead?

260

Relief washes over me.

She won't be able to hurt me anymore. I'm free of her.

Instantly guilt creeps into my heart.

Oh, God.

How can I feel relieved when my mother is dead? What kind of person does that make me?

A war erupts inside me as my emotions burst into a chaotic mess.

"Are you listening!" Bill snaps angrily, and it yanks me back to the call. "Why my daughter put up with you, I'll never understand. The funeral will be held at the Methodist Church on Monday. The least you can do is pay your respects. Make sure you're dressed appropriately as the press will be present. And keep your mouth shut. If you do or say anything to damage my reputation, you'll regret the day you were born."

The call cuts, leaving me with nothing but emptiness on the other side of the line. Slowly my hand drops from my ear to hang limply next to my side.

"Brie?" Colton comes closer, and my eyes lock on him. "Who was that?"

What will Colton think if he knows the first thing I felt was relief? Will he hate me?

261

"My…" Sounding hoarse, I clear my throat before I try again, "My Grandfather."

Colton's features instantly tighten. "What did he want?"

"Wait," Cassie says, and she comes to take hold of my arm. "Sit, Brie. You're as pale as a ghost."

I plop down in the chair, and my gaze drifts to the floor. "My mother died."

"Oh!" Cassie takes a seat at the table and reaching for me, she gives my hand a squeeze. "I'm sorry for your loss, sweetie."

Loss.

Is it a loss, though?

I shut my eyes against the thoughts because they feel wrong. So very wrong.

"She fell down the stairs," I automatically continue. "The funeral is on Monday. He said it will be held at the Methodist Church."

Colton crouches down next to me, placing his hand over mine. "Are you okay?" He pauses for a moment, then hurries to say, "Stupid question. Sorry."

I begin to shake my head, but then my body stills again as I mutter, "How am I supposed to feel?" My eyes lift to Colton's. "I don't know… how…" I shake my head again.

"It's okay to not feel anything right now, Brie," Cassie says, her voice filled with empathy.

My chin begins to tremble from the guilt, and it's hard to whisper the words, "I feel..." Lifting a trembling hand, I cover my mouth as the shock hits.

My mother's dead.

I didn't even say goodbye when I left.

My mind begins to race, bringing up her face as I try to recall anything good. Instead, my memory is filled with animosity.

'Who breaks an arm from a couple of kicks? You're an embarrassment.'

'It's just wood and hair.'

'Damned disgrace! That's all you are.'

'I should've drowned you at birth.'

Colton stands up and pulling me to my feet, his arms tightly envelop me.

My body jerks and I quickly wrap my arms around him as I gasp, "I can't remember anything good." I pull back a little and feel horrible as I admit, "I... I feel... relieved." Saying the words out loud makes me feel like a monster. "I'm an awful person, right?"

Bringing his hands up, Colton frames my face. "You're not, Brie." His eyes capture mine, and I cling to the look of

263

understanding, softening his gaze. "I'd feel relieved as well."

"I think you should both stay home," Cassie says as she gets up. "I'll let the school know."

Colton holds me while Cassie makes the call. When she's done, she turns her gaze to us. "Why don't you both change out of your uniforms." Her eyes go to the untouched bowls of oatmeal. "I'll clear the table."

Colton keeps an arm around me as we leave the kitchen. After walking into my room, Colton rubs his hand gently up and down my back. "Change into something comfortable. Okay?"

I nod, and when he leaves the room, shutting the door, I can only manage to stare blankly in front of me.

I'm more upset about the relief I feel than the fact that my mother is dead.

All she did was break me down. She buried me in abhorrence and cruelty. Not once did she care how I felt.

'I'll drown you.'

'I'll throw you off Devil's Bluff.'

How am I supposed to mourn the person who made my life a living hell?

———————————

COLTON

I change into a pair of sweatpants and a t-shirt and rush out of my room.

Knocking on Brie's door, I wait a moment before I slowly push the door open. She's still standing right where I left her, just staring at nothing.

Walking to her dresser, I open the drawers until I find her sweatpants and pull them out. I also grab a shirt and place the items on the bed before taking hold of Brie's arm. "Come on. Change into these. I'll wait right outside your door."

Her actions are lethargic as she nods while shrugging out of her jacket.

I go to stand outside Brie's room, feeling worried about her. I wish I could just wrap her up in my heart and stop anything from ever hurting her again.

This sucks.

Mom comes up the stairs, and when she reaches me, she whispers, "How are you holding up?"

I shrug. "I'm just worried about Brie. I wish I could make it all better."

"I know." Mom squeezes my arm lovingly. "All you can do is to be there for her."

I nod just as Brie's door opens. Both Mom and my gazes turn to Brie. She first glances at Mom then at me, and her eyes are filled with the same pain they always carried when I met her.

Brie's mother dying, must've yanked the scabs off all her wounds.

Mom reacts before I can and wraps an arm around Brie's shoulders. With everything fresh in Brie's mind, I worry it will make her panic, but instead, she turns into Mom as her face crumbles.

"Shh… everything will be okay," Mom coos.

A sob tears from Brie, and my muscles tighten with the need to comfort her. Guiding Brie back into her room, Mom keeps whispering soothing words. I hear her whisper, "Lie down, sweetie."

No matter how much I want to try to help Brie, deep down, I know she needs my mom more.

I watch them lie down, and Brie curls up into a ball in Mom's arms. Having to do something, I say, "I'll make us some coffee."

Walking to the kitchen, I keep trying to think of a way to make Brie feel better. I make the coffee and placing the mugs on a tray, I carry it to Brie's room and set it down on the bedside table.

Screw this.

I walk around the bed to the side Brie's on and lie down behind her. I place my arm over both of them and press a kiss to Brie's shoulder blade.

God, this is unbearable. Seeing someone you love with all your heart hurt so much is just… torture.

"Cry, sweetie. Let it all out," Mom keeps whispering.

The sun slowly inches its way through the room as we hold Brie.

Chapter 22

BRIE

Dear me,

My mother died. I guess that's why I didn't hear from her again.

Shouldn't I feel bad? Or at least a little sad?

All I feel is... relief. Does that make me a bad person? Does it mean I'm like her?

Her funeral is tomorrow, and I really don't want to go. How am I supposed to mourn someone who never showed me any kind of love?

I only remember the hate. I keep seeing the spite in her eyes and the disdain pulling at her mouth.

I can't remember a single smile.

Not one hug.

Should I pretend to mourn her so people won't judge me for being an awful daughter? There's a burning sensation in the pit of my stomach just thinking about going to the funeral.

I know this makes me an awful person, but at least I'll be done with her once and for all after tomorrow.

I'm sorry I feel this way.

B.

We spent the whole day in bed on Thursday. Friday and yesterday, Colton and I watched one movie after the other while Cassie supplied us with comfort food.

The house, Colton, and Cassie have become a safe haven for me. It feels like as long as I stay here, no one will be able to hurt me.

I sit down on the couch and stare at the coffee table. Memories from the past eighteen years keep haunting me.

"Hey," Colton murmurs as he sits down next to me.

I lean back and hug my legs to my chest. Resting my chin on my knees, I look at Colton. "Hey."

He sits back and turns his body toward me. Lifting a hand, he brushes my bangs away from my eyes. "You know you don't have to go tomorrow, right?"

I nod and let out a sigh. "I'm still in two minds. Part of me wants to forget she ever existed, and the other half wants to go… to get some sort of closure."

Colton seems to think about something for a moment before he says, "Whatever you want to do. We'll go with you."

Worried about my grandparents being there, I murmur, "I've never met my grandparents. I don't know what to say to them."

Colton tilts his head. "They were never a part of your life, Brie. You don't owe them anything, so if you have nothing to say to them, then it's okay. We'll avoid them."

"They paid for our expenses," I admit.

"That doesn't change anything," Colton states.

I let out another sigh, not so sure if Colton is right.

He shifts a little closer to me. "Just because my father is paying for everything doesn't mean shit. It's his damn responsibility. The same counts for your grandparents. They must've known your mother was crazy as hell, and they didn't do anything to help you." Anger tightens his features. "If you ask my opinion, they owe you, Brie. They are the ones who failed you."

My gaze drifts over Colton's features before they settle on his eyes.

His words begin to sink in, and I realize he's right. My grandparents stuck us in this town because they knew my mother was unhinged. All that mattered was their precious public image.

When I was younger, I used to feel sad I never got to see my grandparents. With time, I didn't care anymore.

And now?

For the first time, anger flickers to life.

They rejected me first. They left me with their daughter, knowing how unstable she was.

The anger actually makes me feel better. It's the first emotion that doesn't feel wrong since I got the news of my mother's passing.

"You're right," I whisper. "You'll be there with me so they won't be able to hurt me. At least not physically," I voice another worry.

"And no matter what they say, don't let it get to you. They don't matter in your life, Brie. Just keep telling yourself that," Colton says.

They don't matter.

It's funny how one sentence can change your perception of people. I used to give so many people who didn't matter the power to hurt me.

Michael. Sully. Lindy. All the bullies. None of them have any kind of role in my life. Yet, for too long, I let them walk over me.

Not anymore.

Over the past few weeks, Colton has shown me that I'm worth more than just being someone's punching bag. I do have value. I can be loved.

I'm not worthless.

Emotion wells in my chest, and lifting my head, I take hold of Colton's hand. I interweave our fingers. "Yeah." The corner of my mouth curves slightly up. "You and Cassie are the only people who matter to me."

A smile forms on Colton's face. "Damn right." Lifting my hand, he presses a kiss to my thumb. "The same counts for your mother. Don't feel bad because you're not sad that she's gone. She doesn't deserve your tears. Okay?"

Hearing the words helps lessen the guilt I feel. "Okay."

Staring at Colton, my heart beats a little faster. He's become my world. It happened so quickly it still feels surreal at times.

Without Colton, I'm not so sure I'd still be here today.

She wouldn't have mourned me if I had committed suicide.

The thought rattles through me, and it knocks the breath from my lungs.

"What?" Colton leans closer, concern darkening his eyes.

272

"I just realized something." I shake my head, still feeling overwhelmed by the thought. "My mom threatened to kill me so many times. Even that day, I wanted to commit suicide, she just stood there taunting me." My eyes lock on Colton's. "She wouldn't have cared if I had ended it all."

Wrapping an arm around me, Colton pulls me closer until I can rest my chin on his shoulder. "You're allowed to hate her, Brie. The world is better off with her dead."

The guilt dissipates totally. I think I just needed to hear the words from Colton – to know he won't hate me.

Determined to put my mother in the past, I pull back and say, "I'm not going to feel guilty for being relieved she's gone."

The corners of Colton's lips curve up. "Do you feel better?"

A smile tugs at my mouth. "Yeah." Closing the distance between us again, I wrap my arms around Colton's neck and murmur, "You always make me feel better. Thank you."

COLTON

Even though Brie seems more at ease after we talked, I still worry that things can go epically bad at the funeral.

"Do you want to go for a drive?" I ask her, thinking us getting out of the house for a little while will do her some good.

"Just to drive around?" she asks.

"Yeah." Grinning, I add, "You can show me a couple more places around town."

Brie checks the time on her watch. "It's still early. We could go to Devil's Bluff and maybe walk down one of the trails?"

"Sounds like a good idea."

Brie gets up. "I just want to change into a pair of shorts and put on my sneakers."

"I'll do the same," I say as I climb to my feet.

We dart up to our rooms, and once I've changed into my clothes, I grab my baseball cap and put it on. I also take a backpack from my closet and then go to the kitchen to put a couple of water bottles in it.

Mom walks into the living room, asking, "What's the bag for?"

"Brie and I are going to Devil's Bluff."

"That sounds like a perfect idea," Mom says as she lies down on the couch, then turns on the TV. "I'm going to watch *Emily in Paris*."

"Enjoy."

Brie comes down the stairs and waves at Mom. "See you later."

"Have fun," Mom calls out before her eyes focus on the TV screen.

Brie and I walk to the truck, and once I've reversed out of the driveway, she grins at me. "I'd like to show you the waterfall. Hopefully, there aren't any students from school there."

"From what I've heard, they're all probably sleeping their hangovers off," I mention.

I drive to the spot where I met Michael and park the truck. There's only one other vehicle, so it looks like we got lucky.

Climbing out of the truck, I glance at the backpack. "How far are we going to walk?"

"Not far," Brie points to the trail. "Ten minutes at most, then we'll reach the waterfall."

"Great. I'll leave the water in the truck." Shutting the door, I walk around the back to catch up with Brie. When I hold my hand out to her, there's no hesitation as her fingers wrap around mine.

Walking down the trail, I glance around at our surroundings before looking at Brie. My feelings for her just keep growing, and I was hoping to talk to her about it this weekend, but with her mother dying, I'm not so sure anymore.

It feels like I'm never going to get the chance to ask her to be my girlfriend, and I'm scared we'll end up being nothing more than friends.

"What are you thinking about?" Brie asks, her eyes flitting over my face.

"How nice it is out here," I lie.

I can hear rushing water, and soon the trail opens up to a cove. The waterfall isn't huge, but it sure is pretty, and the pool looks inviting.

We'll have to come back in summer to swim.

"Do you want to sit?" Brie asks, gesturing at a couple of boulders.

"Sure."

We each sit on a boulder, the sound of the waterfall filling the air.

"This is nice," Brie murmurs, a peaceful expression on her face.

"It is." With my eyes on Brie, I think about how much she's changed these past few weeks. She's no longer anxious and smiles more.

"What?" Brie asks when she catches me staring.

"I'm just thinking how much you've changed from the girl I saw on the first day of school."

She gives me a shy grin. "Hopefully, for the better."

"Oh, definitely," I chuckle. "Are you happy?"

The grin turns into a soft smile, and then Brie nods. "Yeah." She scoots off the boulder and walks to the edge of the pool. I watch her pick up a couple of pebbles, and she begins to toss them into the water. "I've never been so happy before."

She turns her face up to the sky, and it reminds me of the sketch she drew of herself.

It also reminds me of the one she drew of her screaming, and it has me asking, "Have you ever yelled?"

"Huh?" She turns to look at me.

"Remember that sketch of you screaming?"

Brie nods.

I glance around, then explain, "There's no one here. Scream."

"Nooo," she laughs, looking awkward.

"Why not?" I ask, climbing to my feet.

277

"Cause I'll look stupid." Her cheeks begin to turn pink, and it makes me smile.

"Have you ever done something you wanted to do?" Brie's smile begins to falter, and it has me asking another question, "If you could do anything right now, what would it be?"

Brie's eyes dart to mine, and I see her hesitate.

"Come on, Brie. What would you do?"

She draws her bottom lip between her teeth, still faltering.

"Okay." I let out a deep breath. "What is one thing you really want to do?"

"Why?" she asks.

"Because I want you to do just one thing for yourself," I explain. A nervous look flitters over her face, and it has me encouraging her, "Just once, Brie. Do something you really want to do."

"What if I do, and it gets me in trouble?"

"As long as we're not going to break any laws, I'm all for it," I say, letting out a chuckle.

"And you won't get angry?" she asks, the corner of her mouth twitching nervously.

"Nope."

"Promise?" she whispers.

278

She's starting to look really anxious, and it makes me wonder what it could be. Hoping I'll set her at ease, I reply, "I promise nothing you want to do will upset me. It will make me happy, Brie. Damn, I'd even jump in the pool with you."

"Okay." She sucks in a deep breath of air and shakes out her hands at her sides. When she starts walking toward me, I expect her to take my hand so we can go do whatever she wants to. But instead, when she reaches me, she lifts herself on her tiptoes, and framing my jaw, she presses her mouth to mine.

Holy shit.

All my brain activity comes to a screeching halt. I don't even have time to respond, and the kiss ends way too quick. Brie takes a couple of steps backward, and her gaze anxiously settles on mine.

Okay, that's seriously the last thing I expected her to do, and it takes me a couple of seconds to get over the initial shock.

Then it hits me. Brie just kissed me.

Our eyes are still locked, and I have to clear my throat before I can ask, "That's the one thing you wanted to do most?"

She nods, and an apologetic look begins to tighten her features. "I… I'm so –" I don't want her saying the words, and darting forward, I frame her face and lower my mouth to hers.

This time I'm prepared, and I get to take in the feel of her lips, how soft and full they are. I breathe in her scent, and tilting my head, I finally allow myself to act on everything I feel for her.

I move as close to her as I can get, and lowering my one hand to the back of her neck, I let my tongue brush over the seam of her mouth. The moment Brie's lips part and I get to taste her, the sound of the waterfall fades until I can only hear my heart thumping against my ribs.

Chapter 23

BRIE

I've thought a lot about how it would feel to kiss Colton, but nothing my imagination conjured up compares to this moment.

None of the emotions come close to what I'm experiencing.

I feel as light as a feather. My heart's fluttering like a pair of butterfly wings between my chest and my throat. My skin's alive with tiny sparks.

It all grows a million times more intense when Colton's tongue slips into my mouth. It's so... so incredible I forget how to breathe.

I somehow manage to lift my hands so I can grab hold of his sides.

I don't get to wonder if I'm doing it right. I don't get to think about what this means.

There's only Colton, and my heart bursting into a kaleidoscope butterflies.

Even though the moment is the most intense thing I've ever felt, it's also so quiet. It's as if we're whispering our feelings through the kiss.

When Colton's mouth slows against mine before he pulls back, I can only suck in air.

Opening my eyes, our gazes lock. The brown of his irises looks like melted chocolate, and his breaths are just as fast as mine. We don't step away from each other, and when the corner of Colton's mouth begins to lift, my heart skips a happy beat.

Moments pass before Colton whispers, "I didn't see that coming. I sure as hell hoped for it, but damn, you just about knocked my feet from under me."

"You hoped for it?" I ask, not able to believe even after the kiss that Colton would actually want me. Yes, it was my dream – one I wished desperately would come true – but never thought would.

"Yeah," he murmurs.

I can only stare at him, my lips parted as hope hovers in my chest.

"So..." Colton's one hand is still on the back of my neck, while his other rests tenderly against my cheek. "I've wanted to tell you how I feel for a while now but could never find the right time."

The fluttering returns full force to my insides, and I nervously lick my lips before asking, "How you feel? About me?"

Colton nods, and his mouth curves into a soft smile. "Yeah." His eyes drift over my face, and the expression in them makes my hope grow. Then he lets out an awkward-sounding chuckle and admits, "I'm falling in love with you."

A smile wavers around my lips, and as his words settle deep in my heart, it grows until happy laughter bubbles out of me. Wrapping my arms around his waist, I squeeze him as tight as I can and whisper, "I'm also falling in love with you."

It's the first time I get to tell someone that I love them, and the moment fills me until it feels like I can't contain all the emotions, and it pushes tears up my throat. A sob flutters over my lips, and I tighten my hold on Colton.

He lowers his head and presses a kiss on my neck, then whispers, "You mean so much to me, Brie."

Hearing the words again opens the floodgates. I never knew how good it would feel. I didn't know how much I needed to hear them.

Colton pulls back, and bringing his hands to my face, he wipes the tears away with his thumbs, an affectionate look softening his features. The expression makes me feel like I'm all he sees.

No one's ever looked at me like that, and I drink it in like someone who's been dying of thirst.

This moment between us feels magical. It's as if anything I wish for can come true, and it's all because of Colton. With him, I'm braver.

"I'm so glad you came to Black Mountain. You've changed everything." Emotion pushes up my throat, and I take a moment to regain control before I continue, "I never want to live in a world you're not in."

Drinking in every inch of his face, I still can't believe he just walked into my life and fought for me. He yanked me out of the nightmare my life was and made me feel safe and loved.

Colton lowers his head, and I instantly push up on my toes to meet his mouth halfway. When our lips touch, Colton sweeps me away to a place where there's only us. It's a wonderland where there's no fear and pain. Only warmth and love.

Breaking the kiss, Colton grins down at me. He looks as happy as I feel, and it makes a burst of laughter bubble over my lips.

"You're so beautiful," he murmurs, his voice much lower and deeper than I've ever heard. He brushes my bangs away from my forehead, and his gaze caresses my face. "How did I get so lucky that none of the idiots at school swept you up?"

My eyes lock with his as I whisper, "It's because you're the only one who saw me."

Colton lets out a chuckle. "From the moment I laid eyes on you," he shakes his head, a serious expression tightening his features, "you were all that mattered."

I can't imagine how bad things could've been if he never came into my life. I probably wouldn't be alive today.

"I'm the lucky one," I say, wishing there was a way to show him just how much he means to me. "You saved my life, Colton. I wouldn't be here right now if it weren't for you."

A look I can't name ripples over his face, and it almost looks like he's going to cry, but then he clears his throat and swallows the expression down. "You have no idea how much I needed to hear that." He takes a step closer, pressing his body against mine, and then he feathers a soft kiss over my lips. "You gave me the chance to redeem myself, Brie. Forget falling. I love you."

It takes a moment for me to realize I did something big for Colton, and it makes a wide smile spread over my face. "I love you, too. With all my heart."

Colton hugs me to his chest, and we stand like that for the longest time while the waterfall rushes into the pool and the sun moves across the sky.

COLTON

Brie keeps thinking I saved her, and yeah, there's truth to it. But I don't think she knows what she did for me. I'm not the hero in our story. Brie is.

We're sitting on the grass, and the sun is starting to set when I say, "You're so much stronger than you think. Yeah, I helped, but at the end of the day, it was all you, Brie."

She brushes her palm over some blades of grass, then glances up at me. "Nope." She shakes her head, a constant smile tugging at the corner of her mouth. "You're the one who fought all my battles."

I tilt my head and capturing her eyes, I say, "And you're the one who fought for survival for eighteen years. I only gave you another option, but you were the one who made the choice to move in with us. That's huge, Brie. That's one hell of a leap you took."

I can see my words are getting through to her, but then she says, "Yeah, but it was an easy choice to make because you were there."

"You gave my mom a chance," I remind her, hoping to make her see it was all her.

"Because she's kind like you," she shoots it down.

I shake my head, determined to get through to her. "Brie, what I'm trying to say is that you gave my mom a chance at life. She was..." I shake my head again, "she gave up after Brady died. You got her to leave her room. You gave her a reason to get up every day." I lean forward, my eyes intense on hers. "You gave me my mother back."

Brie's eyes begin to shine, and she swallows hard.

Knowing I'm finally getting her to understand, I continue, "I blamed myself for Brady's death."

Brie instantly begins to shake her head, but I reach for her hand, saying, "Let me finish." When she nods, I admit, "The night Brady committed suicide was the first time I left him alone to face our father."

Sitting with Brie as dusk sets in, I allow my thoughts to return to that night, and the familiar crippling sorrow seeps into my heart.

"Brady was upset because his girlfriend wanted to take their relationship to the next level. He felt he needed to tell her about our father before they did… the deed. But he couldn't. He didn't want her to see him as less. It really got to him."

Understanding settles in Brie's eyes. It's so easy to talk to her because we're kindred souls.

"My father overheard us talking and took it as an opportunity to lay into Brady."

'I told you you'll never be good enough for the likes of Jade Daniels. She needs a man with an actual set of balls and not some pussy.'

The words shudder through me as if my father's here, saying them now. "I'll never forget the hurt on Brady's face, and I know my brother believed every word my father spewed, no matter what I said," I admit to Brie.

'Stop it!' I shout, and taking a step closer to our father, I fist my hands at my sides. 'What the hell is wrong with you? How can you say that to Brady? He's your son!' Enraged by the hurt, he caused my brother, the self-control I always have begins to slip.

"I lost my temper." Lifting my eyes to Brie's face, I see she's totally focused on me before I lower my gaze back to the grass. "I was always the patient one. I took the brunt of his rages so Brady and my mom wouldn't have to. But that night… I lost it."

'Who the hell do you think you are?' he shouts back, spittle flying from his mouth. Raising his arm, he's just about to hit me when I lift my own and block the blow.

*I step right up to him, and we come eye to eye as I hiss, "I'm **your** son. Brady's **your** son.' My body trembles as I cling to the last of my self-restraint. 'You treat us worse than dogs. You're not a man.' I shake my head as disgust for him wells in my chest. 'You're nothing more than a coward who beats his own family.'*

He shoves me back, but I manage to catch myself from losing my balance. Standing my ground, my eyes burn on him with hatred. 'You're nothing but a sick fuck.'

He lets out a growl as he storms me. The force from the blow of his body slamming against mine knocks me into the wall. His fist connects with my side, and it makes a sharp, burning sensation spread through my insides.

"Things got really bad," I murmur as the night keeps playing out in my mind like a bad movie. I let out a heavy breath. "I would've killed him if I I'd stayed at home." I shake my head as the weight of my decision settles heavily on my shoulders. "So, I left. I just walked around the town until I felt calmer." Lifting my eyes to Brie, remorse squeezes at my heart. "By the time I got home, Brady had already shot himself."

Walking up the street I live in, I see emergency lights flashing up ahead. Instantly apprehension ripples through me, and I break out into a run.

Reaching the driveway, a police officer tries to stop me, but shouting, "I live here," I manage to get past him and run over the lawn to the front door.

Fear prickles over my skin, and one thought after the other flash through my mind.

Did he hurt Brady? Or my mother?

Shit, I shouldn't have left.

I dart into the house and up the stairs. The first thing I see is Mom standing by the bathroom with an officer. There are tears streaming down her face, and she looks like she's seen a ghost.

There's no sign of my father, and I hear voices coming from Brady's room. Walking closer, someone says, "You can't go in there."

"It's my brother's room," I snap, pushing past the officer who just addressed me.

My eyes land on the bed, and it takes a long second for the sight to make sense. It looks like Brady's just staring up at the ceiling. Only there's blood. So much blood. The iron scent hangs thick in the air, and it begins to suffocate me, filling my stomach with bile.

I somehow manage to walk a little closer before I'm stopped by an officer. His arm wraps around me as I stare at my brother's lifeless eyes.

When the officer begins to pull me away, my muscles tighten, and I try to yank free to get to Brady. "Let go," I growl as I keep struggling at the hold.

Another officer comes to help, and I don't have the strength to fight them both.

"Get him out of the room," someone snaps.

I start to shake my head, my gaze locked on my brother as the realization that he's dead rips a gaping hole right through my life.

I hear someone shout, and my throat burns as I gasp for air. They pull me backward, and no matter how hard I fight, the distance between Brady and me keeps growing.

"Colton." Brie's soft voice draws me back to the present. She's moved onto her knees and shifted closer to me. Her hand's on my shoulder, and as I raise my eyes to meet hers, she leans forward and hugs me.

Bringing my own arms up, I wrap them around her and pull her onto my lap. Burying my face in her neck, I hold onto her because this girl is the only one who has the power to keep me from drowning.

"I should've stayed and killed the bastard," I murmur, my voice rough from all the grief and anger. "Then Brady would still be here."

Brie pulls back a little, and as she frames my jaw with her hands, her chin trembles. "I know I sound selfish, but if you had killed your father, you would be in prison." A tear spirals over her cheek. "And I wouldn't be here."

Brie's words loosen the tight hold of regret around my heart, and I swallow hard before I admit, "Now do you understand what you mean to me? What you've done for me?"

She nods as her tears begin to fall faster.

"You're the one who saved me, Brie," I whisper before I press my mouth to hers.

Out of all the horror I've suffered, Brie was the one good thing to come from it. Maybe, just maybe, the reason everything happened was so I would see Brie's torment where everyone else was blind to it.

I'll always miss my brother, but I think Brady would be happy if he knew I found Brie because of him.

Even in death, he managed to give me peace and love.

I pull back, and my eyes meet Brie's. "Brady would have liked you."

"I'm sure I would've liked him as well," she replies.

Chapter 24

BRIE

Dear me,

I have so many happy feelings, but I don't know how to write them down.

We kissed!!! Colton's lips were on mine. More than once. He also said he loves me. We talked until it was dark, and I'm just writing this down quickly before dinner because I don't want to forget.

I've never been this happy. It feels like it's bursting out of me and shining like a second sun.

Colton told me about the night Brady died. I never knew how much Colton blamed himself, and at least I got to help him in some way. It makes me feel closer to him. It's like we're two pieces of the same soul. I wish I could explain it better.

I guess the only thing that matters is our love. Colton is my everything.

B.

Ps. Does this mean we're dating now? Should I ask him?

Waking up and feeling Colton's chest rise and fall beneath my cheek, a smile spreads over my face.

Last night we talked about everything we could think of until we fell asleep. I learned the reason why Colton has to redo his senior year. Hearing what he's been through makes my own past feel… less traumatic.

I lift my head and stare down at his sleeping face. It's mind-blowing how just in a few weeks, everything has changed. When Colton walked into school, I was sure he'd become another bully. Instead, he turned out to be my hero.

The love of my life.

He begins to grin, then sleepily murmurs, "I can feel you staring."

I let out a chuckle, and climbing over him, I get up. "I'll make us some coffee."

Walking to the bathroom first, the thought settles hard in my stomach today is my mother's funeral. I still feel apprehensive about meeting my grandparents. But, I've decided to go so I can say goodbye to my mother. I'm doing it for myself because it's my way of shutting the door on my past.

Everything will be okay. Colton and Cassie will be there.

After relieving myself and brushing my teeth, I go to my room and quickly pull a brush through my hair, then I walk down to the kitchen. I see Colton's still lying on the couch and wonder if he dozed off again.

I start to make coffee as Cassie comes down the stairs. When she sees me, she says, "Morning, sweetie. How do pancakes sound for breakfast?"

"Yummy," I grin.

Colton gets up from the couch, and my eyes drift over his tousled hair and the scruff on his jaw as he walks toward the stairs.

Yep, definitely yummy.

I feel the heat creep up my neck and quickly carry on making coffee. Still, a broad smile spreads over my face.

Cassie gathers all the ingredients she'll need, and I move her cup closer. "Here you go."

"Thank you." I lean back against the counter and sip on the warm liquid. When Colton comes into the kitchen, I point at his cup. "There's yours."

"Thanks." He shoots me a grin before picking up his coffee. He comes to stand right next to me, also leaning against the counter. We glance at each other, and it makes a blush spread over my cheeks.

It's still unbelievable that we kissed yesterday.

Cassie's gaze drifts over us, and when she tilts her head, frowning at us, I quickly lift the mug to hide the smile on my face behind it.

"Did I miss something?" she asks, a teasing tone to her voice.

Colton lets out a chuckle, then he whispers to me, "We might as well tell her now."

My eyes widen as I look up at him. "Huh?"

"Brie and I..."

Nooooo.

I quickly put the cup down and then cover Colton's mouth with my hand. My eyes dart from him to Cassie, then back to him, and standing on my toes, I whisper right by his ear, "You can't tell your mom we kissed."

Colton begins to laugh, and pulling my hand away, he says, "I wasn't going to." He places his arm around my shoulder and pulls me against his side. "Isn't she cute?" he asks Cassie.

She nods, silently laughing as her eyes never leave us. "I'm going to take a wild guess here. Are the two of you a couple?"

Colton begins to nod. "Yeah." Then he turns his gaze to me. "Right?"

I let out a chuckle. "Definitely."

Cassie lets out a squeak and rushing over to us, she hugs us. "I'm so happy." When she pulls back, she turns her attention back to the pancakes, a contented smile on her face.

I glance up at Colton and don't have any time to stop him as he presses a quick kiss to my mouth. Again my eyes widen, and I hiss, "Your mom."

"You don't mind, right, Mom?" Colton asks, and it sends my face up in flames.

"If you kiss?" Cassie asks playfully. "Not at all. But when things get serious, just remember to use protection."

Oh, my God. I'm just going to die right now.

I let out a groan and cover my burning cheeks with my hands, making them both laugh.

———

I've decided to wear a navy blue dress and a white cardigan. In a way, it feels like I'm rebelling by not wearing traditional black for the funeral.

Walking down the stairs, I come to a stop when I see Colton, dressed in black suit pants and a white button-up shirt. I watch him shrug on the jacket over his broad shoulders.

He doesn't look like a senior, but instead a man. A very attractive man. There's a weird sensation in my abdomen, and slapping a hand over it, I slowly walk closer.

"Are you ready?" he asks when he notices me.

"Yeah."

Cassie comes rushing down the stairs, checking her purse. "I think I have everything." Then her eyes fall on me. "You look so pretty."

"Thank you." I gesture at the black dress she's wearing. "You look pretty, as well."

"Okay, let's do this," Colton says, and sucking in a deep breath, he opens the front door.

We walk to his truck, and when he opens the passenger door, he murmurs, "Ladies."

"You can sit in the middle, Brie." Cassie nudges my back lightly.

Getting in, I scoot up to make space for Cassie. Once we're all in the cab, and Colton puts the truck in reverse, the back of his hand brushes against my knee. It sends sparks racing over my skin.

"Goosebumps," he whispers before placing his arm behind me so he can pull the vehicle out of the driveway.

I shouldn't be grinning like an idiot right now, but I can't help it. Sitting so close to him has all the butterflies throwing a party in my stomach.

I'm so going to hell.

"Can you stop at the flower shop? I want to get fresh ones for Brady," Cassie says, and it instantly changes the vibe in the cab from happy to sad.

"Sure."

My eyes dart up to Colton's face, and when I see the hard line of grief around his mouth, I move my hand from my lap to his thigh. His hand instantly covers mine.

Colton pulls up to the store, and while Cassie runs inside, he leans down and presses a soft kiss to my mouth. His lips linger on mine for a couple of seconds before he lifts his head. "How are you holding up?"

"Good." I scrunch my nose. "I'd rather be home watching movies, but…" I let out a sigh, then ask, "And you?"

"I'd also rather watch movies." He grins. "Lying on the couch with you. Stealing kisses."

I smile back at him. "I meant, how do you feel about going to the cemetery? Are you okay with it?"

Colton nods, and his eyes dart over to the sidewalk before they come back to me. "I'll be okay. Plus, I think it's a good opportunity to introduce you to Brady."

Cassie opens the passenger door, and I take the bouquet of lilies from her, so she can climb in.

A couple of minutes later, Colton parks outside the Methodist church. I watch as people I've never seen before walk into the building.

Cassie opens the door, and it has me asking, "Can we wait until everyone's inside?"

"Sure."

A weird feeling spreads through my chest as I watch everyone go inside, and I mutter, "So many people. Did any of them even know my mother, or are they here for my grandparents?"

"Probably here for the press," Colton replies as he points toward the news vans.

"That's not good," Cassie adds. "Stick between Colton and me. If any of them start asking you questions, we'll leave right away."

"Okay."

When the sidewalk is quieter, we climb out. Crossing the road, I ask, "Can we sit in the back somewhere?"

"Of course."

Colton takes the lead as we near the church. It's cold inside, and I'm glad I'm wearing a cardigan. My gaze darts over the rows filled with strangers, and knowing my grandparents will be upfront, my eyes settle on the couple in the first row.

I expected to feel something... anything, but instead, there's nothing as I look at them. Colton takes my hand and pulls me into the second last row, where we take a seat.

A preacher clears his throat and begins to welcome everyone. My eyes go to the massive portrait of my mom that's standing next to the coffin. She's smiling in the photo, and even though there's a haughty gleam in her eyes, the smile seems real.

I keep staring at her eyes, waiting for the guilt to return. But instead, all I feel is uneasy.

There really isn't anything good I can remember of her.

You hurt me. You made me feel worthless.

I won't miss you.

Bye, Mom.

When the service is over, we slip out the doors as the other people get up from their seats. Once we're in the truck, I take a relieved breath.

If Cassie didn't get flowers for Brady's grave, I'd ask them if we could just go home. Instead, I keep quiet as Colton steers the vehicle in the direction of the cemetery.

We're the first ones there, and after climbing out, Colton and I follow Cassie to where Brady is. Colton's hand finds mine, and he interweaves our fingers tightly.

My eyes dart over the words on the headstone. He was only sixteen.

Sadness fills my heart because his life ended so soon. I'm sure he would've been just as happy as I am if he had held out.

"Sorry for only coming now, my baby," Cassie whispers as she sets the flowers down by the headstone. "I miss you so much."

Tears well in my eyes, and I struggle to blink them away.

Cassie glances at us and tearfully says, "Brady's smile could warm the coldest day."

"Yeah," Colton murmurs. Tugging at my hand, he leads me away, then says, "Give her some time alone with him. We can come back another time."

"Are you sure?" I ask, not wanting to keep Colton from Cassie and Brady.

"Yeah, it's her first time here since we buried him."

"Have you been visiting him?" I ask.

Colton nods. "I still struggle… leaving him alone."

I give his hand a squeeze and then notice all the people from the church gathering around the fresh gravesite. "We can just stand to the side."

"Okay."

We stop under a tree, and I watch as my grandfather and other men carry the coffin. His eyes are red as if he's been crying.

I guess even monsters have someone who mourns them.

The preacher says a couple of words, and as they start to lower the coffin, my grandfather gets up and surprises me by walking toward me. I didn't think he saw me.

His eyes are green, like my mother's. Just as cold, as well.

"So you're Brie," he grumbles, a sneer around his mouth as if he just tasted something terrible.

"Yes."

Colton tightens his hold on my hand as my grandfather's gaze sweeps over me. "I should've known you'd disobey me. I now understand why your mother always complained about you. You can't even wear black for her funeral."

I stare at the old man, and with Colton next to me, I feel braver than ever. "I figured black is for when you're grieving. I have nothing to mourn."

My grandfather lets out a bitter chuckle that sounds more like a bark. "That my poor daughter had to raise..." his eyes snap over me with disgust, "you. I should've forced her to give you up for adoption."

"You should've," I agree. Maybe then I would've had a happy life from the start.

He shakes his head and then digs a piece of paper out of the inside pocket of his jacket. "Here." I take it from him, a frown settling on my forehead. "I never want to hear your name again. Stay out of the media and our lives."

Without another glance, he walks away. I pull my hand free from Colton's and open the paper, and then my eyes grow wide. It's a check for one million dollars. "Holy crap." I turn my stunned gaze to Colton, who looks just as surprised as me. "I should give it back. Right?"

Colton's eyes dart between my hands and my face, but before he can answer, Cassie comes to stand by us. She looks at the amount on the check then says, "You should keep it, Brie. Take it as payment for years of hell being stuck with his daughter."

"Won't it be wrong of me?" I ask, not sure I should take any money from him.

"Not at all," Cassie says. "You don't have to spend it now. You can invest it, and one day when you realize how much you deserve that money, you can use it."

It sure would help with my personal expenses, so I don't have to depend on Cassie and Colton for everything. I look at the amount again. I can even donate most of it to a good cause if it bothers me so much.

I hold the check out to Cassie and ask, "Can you keep it for me. I'm scared I'll lose it."

I watch her tuck it in her purse before I glance at my mother's grave. A reporter catches my eye, and as she takes a step toward us, I say, "We better go. A reporter is heading our way."

We begin to walk away, and then Cassie glances over her shoulder. "Shit, she's catching up. Let's run."

We all dart forward, and Colton's taller, so he keeps tugging at my hand. Then Cassie passes us, letting out a burst of laughter, which makes me chuckle.

We all bundle into the truck, and Colton quickly drives away. With a smile, I glance out the back window and watch the reporter shake her head.

Turning my gaze to the front, my eyes meet Cassie's, and impulsively I ask, "Will it be okay if I called you Mom?"

Her smile widens, and she pulls me into a hug. "It would make me so happy. I always wanted a daughter."

When she pulls back, I say, "You're the best mother I could've asked for."

"As long as you both know we're first going to finish our studies before there's any talk of marriage," Colton suddenly says.

I look like a gaping fish while Cassie laughs, "Who said anything about getting married?"

"Just saying," Colton shrugs, then he playfully grins at us. "Also, it looked like you were both about to cry, and I thought dropping a bomb would stop the floodgates from opening."

Our laughter fills the cab as Colton drives us home, and then my thoughts turn back to Cassie. The moment just felt so right, and honestly, she really is the only mother I've ever known. I know it's sudden, but for me, it feels natural.

I also know it's weird that it happened after Serena's funeral, but I guess she did more for me by dying than she ever did while alive.

Chapter 25

COLTON

Brie's been staring at the check since we got home. Her facial expressions keep alternating between determination and doubt.

Sitting down on the couch next to her, I ask, "What's going on in that head of yours?"

Her eyes dart to mine before they return to the piece of paper. "I can't decide whether I should keep it or tear it up." She shifts her body, so she faces me, then asks, "What would I do with so much money?"

"Anything you want to do," I reply. "You can pay for college."

She nods. "Still, at most, I only need ten percent of it."

"Then invest the rest, like Mom said."

A grin spreads over her face. "*Mom*. I like that."

"Me too," Mom chuckles as she walks into the kitchen. "What do you want for dinner?"

"Mac and cheese," I call out.

"Mac and cheese, it is then."

While Mom starts with dinner, Brie moves closer to me and whispers, "Don't you think we should take Mom for a picnic to the waterfall on Sunday?"

My eyebrows raise at the idea. "Yeah, she'll love that."

"We can make sandwiches and get some muffins or cupcakes from the store."

"Sounds good to me."

When Brie's eyes turn back to the check, I pull the paper out of her hand. "You don't have to decide today. Let's watch something." Getting up, I walk to the kitchen and hand the check to Mom, then I pour us all some soda while asking, "Brie, What do you feel like watching?"

"Maybe something to do with college?"

"Oooh!" Mom almost starts jumping from excitement. "Let's watch After."

I let out a sigh. "Romance it is." I place a glass on the counter near Mom and give her a grateful smile. She was really fantastic today. "Thank you for today."

Mom taps her cheek with her pointer finger, and after I give her a kiss, she says, "You can start the movie. I'll watch from here."

"You sure? We can wait."

She gestures toward Brie with her eyes. "Go cuddle her. I know you're dying to."

Shaking my head, I let out a chuckle as I carry the other two glasses to the living room. I set them down on the coffee table, and reaching for the remote, I turn on the TV.

When I press play, Brie snuggles up to my side, and I place my arm around her shoulders. After a couple of minutes, she murmurs, "Today was so different from what I expected."

"It's because you were prepared for the worse."

"True."

As I watch the girl on the screen walk to her class, I mention, "Enjoy tonight because tomorrow we have a lot of school work to catch up on."

"Ugh, did you have to remind me?" Brie complains.

Chuckling, I kiss her temple. Brie lifts her head and first glances at the kitchen before she presses a quick kiss to my lips.

———————————

It took us three days to catch up with the work we missed, but as we sit down for dinner, I feel better knowing it's done.

I made us chicken and salad tonight because Mom's been cooking for the past week.

Just as Brie pops a piece of meat in her mouth, there's a knock at the door.

Frowning, I get up. "I'll get it."

"Probably the wrong house," Mom mumbles around a piece of tomato.

I open the door, and instantly the blood drains from my face.

"Hello, son. Aren't you going to let me in?"

I hear a chair scrape over the tiles from the kitchen, and glancing toward the sound, I see Mom heading toward us, and I snap. "Stay with Brie!"

Shoving my father backward, I step out onto the porch and shut the front door behind me. When my eyes focus on his face, a rage, unlike anything I've felt before, sets fire to the blood rushing through my veins. "What the hell are you doing here?"

He gives me a condescending smirk. "I'm here to bring my wife and son back home."

"Like hell you are," I growl, fisting my hands at my sides. "Get off our property."

He lets out an arrogant chuckle. "My property. I'm paying for this house." He tries to step by me. "Let's talk inside."

"No!" I shove him back again. "You're not setting foot inside this house. Leave. It's my last warning."

Anger begins to simmer in his eyes. "And then? What? Have you grown a set the past four months?" He takes a threatening step closer to me. "Mind if I check?"

What the fuck?

The same old crazy look settles over his face when he sees my reaction. "Yeah, just like I thought. Once a pussy, always a pussy. Get out of my way before I beat your ass."

That's all it takes for rage to consume me, and I lunge forward. My fist slams into this jaw, and as he staggers backward, I follow.

"Colton! Stop!" I hear Mom scream, but ignoring her, I begin to deliver one punch after the other.

For Brady. For Mom. For myself.

Years of anger pour out of me as I watch blood flow from my father's nose, and I grind the words out through clenched teeth, "It hurts, doesn't it?"

He begins to drag himself away from me, and holding up a hand, he begs, "Stop. Please. Stop."

All the fight drains from me as I stare down at the pathetic mess on the ground. "Funny how you never cared when we begged you to stop."

"You broke my nose," he complains, covering his face with a trembling hand.

"Yeah? You broke my ribs." Taking a step closer to him, I snap, "Do you really want to compare injuries? Because then, I better start beating your sorry ass again."

My father climbs to his feet, and his eyes dart to Mom. "Are you just going to stand there and do nothing?"

Mom moves to my side. "I think Colton is handling this well."

He lets out a frustrated huff. "Always hiding behind him. Some fucking mother you are."

Stepping in front of Mom, I glare darkly at him. "Leave before I keep my promise and put you in the ICU."

Disgust ripples over his bloody face. "That's it. I'm cutting you both off. You're dead to me, just like Brady."

Mom grabs hold of my arm when I want to dart forward. "Let him leave."

He shakes his head at us one last time, and with a careless wave that shows he's done with us, he walks to his car.

I wait until his car disappears from sight before I turn to Mom. "Are you okay?"

She nods, and her bottom lip juts out as she takes hold of my right hand. "Look at your knuckles. Let's go inside so we can clean the blood off."

Walking to the front door, I notice Brie standing on the porch, her face pale. I dart forward and taking hold of her shoulders, I say, "I'm sorry you had to see that."

Brie shakes her head and wraps her arms around my neck, hugging me tightly. "I'm just glad he's gone." She pulls back, and her eyes lock with mine. "Are you okay?"

I wait for Mom and Brie to walk into the house and shutting the door, I say, "I am now."

It felt good standing up for myself for once and getting rid of the pent up anger. Now that I've fought back, he'll hopefully stay away.

When I walk to the bathroom, Mom and Brie follow behind me. I let Mom clean my hand, knowing she needs to do it. Also, I love having her fuss over me.

"I'll make an appointment to meet with a lawyer," Mom murmurs. "It's time to divorce him."

"I can help with money," Brie suddenly says. When we look at her, she rambles, "I overheard what he said, and I don't want you worrying about finances."

315

Mom wipes the last of the blood away, then turns and drops the cloth in the sink before turning to Brie. "You're going to invest that money, Brie. I spent twenty-two years with that man, and he'll pay for every one of them."

"Okay," Brie replies. "I just wanted you to know, I don't mind helping."

Mom pulls Brie into a hug. "Thank you, sweetie." When they pull apart, Mom adds, "We'll go to the bank tomorrow after school. Okay?"

"Yeah."

Mom glances back at me. "I'm going to heat the chicken so we can finish having dinner."

Once she leaves, Brie moves closer to me. She takes hold of my hand and presses a kiss to the back of it. "It looks like it's going to swell. Does it hurt?"

I shake my head and lift my left hand to her face, brushing her bangs away from her eyes. "Are you okay?"

Brie nods. "You were handling it, so I wasn't scared. I knew you'd take care of it."

The corner of my mouth lifts at hearing how much trust she has in me.

Brie's eyes search my face. "Are you really okay?"

"Yeah. I wasn't while he was here, but now…" I shake my head, "I need to show him I'm not scared of him. I'm fine now."

Brie looks at my hand again. "Let's put some ice on your knuckles."

We go to the kitchen, and while Brie grabs a pack of frozen peas, I head to where Mom's heating the chicken in the microwave. I place a hand on her back and wait until she looks at me. "Do you want me to go with you to the lawyers?"

She shakes her head, giving me a comforting smile. "I'll be fine. It's not like he'll be there." Mom gestures to Brie. "Go sit and ice your hand while I finish up here."

Once we're all seated, my gaze moves between the two women in my life, and knowing I protected them from my father fills my chest with pride.

Chapter 26

BRIE

Dear me,

Colton's dad showed up. Things didn't go well. Actually, it was terrible, and I shouldn't be glad Colton hit his father, but I can't help it. After everything that man put them through, he deserved that beating and more.

I know Cassie is worried about money and that Mr. Lawson will stop sending any, but she shouldn't. I've made up my mind to take the money from my grandfather. I'll look after Cassie and Colton the same way they looked after me.

I hope he never comes here again.

B.

———————————

"There's an art competition at the University of Black Mountain," I tell Colton on the way to school. "With everything that happened, I forgot to mention it."

"Yeah? Are you going to enter?" he asks as he steers the truck through the morning traffic.

"I want to. I'm not sure what to draw, though," I admit.

There's a moment's silence, then Colton mentions, "You're really good at expressing emotions. Maybe draw something that relates to how you feel now?"

I begin to nod as ideas stream into my head. "Yeah, that's a good idea." I worry my bottom lip while I think, and then ask, "Maybe something to do with love?"

"Like a heart?" Colton pulls into the parking area and finds a space to stop the truck.

"Maybe more like darkness spreading out into light? A lot of shades?" The more I think about it, the more an image begins to form in my minds-eye. "Or hope? A chain of butterflies breaking?"

Colton turns the truck off and looks at me. "I really like that idea."

"Yeah?" Happy that I finally have something to work with, I grin as I push open the door and climb out.

We meet at the front of the vehicle, and Colton takes hold of my hand then presses a slow kiss to my lips. "I'm sure it's going to be a masterpiece."

Lifting on my toes, I press another kiss to his mouth before we start to walk toward the building.

With all the faith Colton has in me, it feels like I can do anything.

The day is just like any other. Lindy made a snide comment about me killing Serena, but weirdly it didn't get to me like it would've in the past.

There's so much truth to what Colton said the other day – I shouldn't let people who don't matter upset me.

After school, we go pick up Mom then stop at the bank so I can open an account and deposit the check with them. The process takes forever, but I know it has to be done. The instant we get home, I change into comfortable clothes, and taking my art supplies, I go sit on the floor in the living room. I position my sketchpad and pencils on the coffee table, and soon, I'm lost in my drawing.

Colton comes to lie on the couch with a book, and it makes the corner of my mouth lift.

This is nice. Us just doing our own thing.

When it begins to grow dark, Mom turns on the light. She gives us a loving smile then goes to prepare dinner.

I manage to complete the sketch minutes before dinner is ready and stretch my arms out above my head.

Then I hear Colton say, "Wow, you're definitely winning with that sketch."

I look at what I've drawn, then grin at Colton. "Yeah? You think so?"

"I know so," he states as he gets up from the couch. He holds a hand out to me, and when I place mine in his, he pulls me to my feet, then folds me in a hug. "I have a talented girlfriend. Lucky me."

I glance at the kitchen, and seeing Mom's back is turned to us, I quickly steal a kiss before we set the table.

Mom places the lasagna on the table, and once we've all scooped some into our plates, she asks, "I think you should both go check out the campus before you decide to enroll."

"That's a good idea," Colton agrees.

My gaze darts to him. "Mom said both of us. Does that mean you're going to study further?"

He thinks about it for a moment, then answers, "Yeah, but I have no idea what to study. Definitely nothing office related. I'll die if I have to sit at a desk and stare at the screen all day."

"What about something where you get to work with people?" Mom mentions.

"You'll be great with people," I comment. Excitement builds in my chest, and then I begin to ramble, "I've dreamt about opening an art healing center. You know, a place where people who have difficult home lives can come to express themselves? Maybe if you study something along the lines of social work, then you can help them?" I suck in a deep breath of air and finish, "Like you helped me."

Mom and Colton stare at me, and then a smile begins to spread over Colton's face. "I really like the sound of that."

"Yes," Mom agrees. "And you have the money now to get the art healing center off the ground."

I grin like a happy fool, and we all begin to mention ideas of how we can make it happen. We discuss what the center can look like and suitable areas we can look at property.

My heart feels like it's going to burst as my dream begins to take shape with Colton and Mom's support.

COLTON

322

It's been two weeks since I decided to study social work, and we're taking Mom's advice to visit the campus before we enroll.

Yesterday, Mom and her lawyer left to attend a settlement meeting in California. Hopefully, they can come to an agreement, and the divorce can be finalized. I'd hate for it to be a long dragged out fight in court. I wanted to go with, but Mom wouldn't hear of it, saying this is a battle she has to fight on her own.

I still don't like it, but I take some comfort that the lawyer will be with her. Also, I get to be alone with Brie. Last night I made us nachos, and we started binge-watching *The Flash*.

Fine, so we spent most of the night making out and didn't take in much of what was happening on TV. It's just... I can't get enough of kissing Brie, and my emotions keep growing stronger. But I want to take things slow with her. I want to enjoy every kiss, every touch, and not just go from one to one hundred in a single day.

I want to treasure what we have.

Driving to the university, I pick up Brie's hand from where it was resting on my thigh and press a kiss to her knuckles, then ask, "Are you excited?"

She grins, her blue eyes sparkling like sapphires. "Yes! I can't wait. This is going to be so amazing."

I let out a chuckle, loving her reaction. It's infectious, making my heartbeat speed up. "I'm glad it's close enough to home, and we don't have to leave Mom alone."

"Yeah, we can commute like we're doing with school now," Brie agrees.

"We'll save money by not having to pay for housing," I add.

Brie nods, and when I steer the truck into a parking area, her eyes dart over our surroundings, murmuring, "It's massive."

Once I've parked the truck, we climb out and interweaving our fingers, we both grin happily as we walk to a vast expanse of lawn.

"I love all the trees," Brie gasps as she continues to drink in our surroundings.

"I think that's the administration office," I mention as I gesture toward a modern building to our left. Entering the office space, there's a line, and we have to wait five minutes before we can get brochures and find out where the relevant classes are situated on campus.

Our enthusiasm keeps growing as we walk around, taking in all the students and getting swept up in the feel of college life.

We spend our entire Friday afternoon on the campus and even stop at the coffee house to each get a bagel and cappuccino.

"I can get used to this," I murmur before I take a bite.

"Mmh-hhm," Brie mumbles around her food, and then she groans, "So nice."

Like a typical guy, one eyebrow pops up at hearing the sound, and all brain activity is redirected to my cock.

I have to shake my head and clear my throat to get out of the trance, long enough to mutter, "When you're done, we can head home."

"Okay."

I scarf down the rest of my bagel, and the instant Brie's done, I discard our trash and drag her to the truck.

When I open the passenger door, Brie asks, "What's the hurry?"

"It's our last night before Mom's back," I explain. I wait for Brie to climb in, then shut the door and walk around the front. Sliding behind the steering wheel, I continue, "Which means it's our last night to make out."

A burst of laughter explodes from Brie. "Now, I get it." While I reverse the truck, Brie scoots closer to me, and making air-quotes with her fingers, she teases, "So we're watching *'The Flash'* again?"

"Not a chance in hell," I chuckle.

———————————

I manage to regain control over my hormones during the drive home. That's until Brie leans back against my chest. We're sitting on the floor, and my back is resting against the couch. Shit, I can't focus on *The Flash* even if my life depended on it.

I pull one arm free from where it's wrapped around her and placing my hand on her shoulder, I lightly run my fingers down to her wrist, just wanting to touch her.

She's so damn soft. Like silk.

I lower my head, and when my breath skims against her neck, goosebumps spread out over her skin.

With the show totally forgotten, I drink in her every reaction to me touching her.

Again, I trail my fingers up and down the length of her arm. My lips curve up when more goosebumps follow my fingers. I move my hand to her hip and brush it along the side of her leg, to her knee, and then back again.

I'm entranced by her response to my touch. I pull my other hand free and bring it to her jaw. Turning her face toward me, I let my breath fan over her jaw.

Her hands drop to my thighs, and she grips hold of the fabric of my sweatpants.

My mouth brushes down her neck to where her pulse is racing, and I groan, "I want to touch you." My hand moves from the outside of her knee to the inside. "Can I?"

Brie nods and murmurs, "Okay." As I slide my fingers down between her legs, her breaths flutter over her lips.

When I cover her mound, the heat I feel coming from her makes my eyes drift shut. I begin to rub my palm against her, and as her breaths start to come faster, I move my other hand to her breast.

Awareness of how womanly she is, shudders through me. It's taking all my control to keep my touch gentle, and I clench my teeth.

An overwhelming need to consume her almost robs me of my self-restraint, and for a moment, my touch grows harder. I squeeze her breast, and my palm rubs feverishly between her legs.

By some miracle, I manage to regain some control over the need coursing through my veins, and I slow my movements. Knowing it's the first time she's being touched like this, I want to make it special for her.

I press a kiss to her pulse, and feeling how madly it's beating, I move my hand to the band of her sweatpants and slip it under the fabric. Brie's breaths race over her parted lips, her eyes hooded by her lashes. I let my fingers run along the seam of her panties before I push beneath them.

When I cover her again, Brie's breaths hitch in her throat, and her eyes drift shut. With no clothing between us, the heat coming off her scorches my willpower to ashes.

"God," I groan from deep in my throat.

Brie's fingers dig into my thighs, and she tilts her head back, exposing all of her neck to me and thrusting her breast into my palm.

I quickly move my hand under her shirt, and pulling her bra out of the way, I palm her breast. Feeling how hard her nipple is against my skin makes a shudder ripple through my body.

I'm so hard for this girl, and I've passed the point of caring whether she can feel it against her lower back.

Spreading her, my fingers glide over her clit, and it sends another shudder filled with need through me.

Brie begins to rub her hands up and down my thighs, and I wish she was rubbing something else.

"Shit, you feel so good," I murmur before my mouth latches onto her pulse, and I begin to suck at her skin like a starved man.

Slipping my hand further down, I slowly push a finger inside her, reveling in how tight she feels.

All mine.

I rub my palm hard against her clit as I push in deeper.

She's all mine.

A soft moan drifts over her parted lips, and she turns her face to mine. I trail kisses up her neck and over her jaw, then soak in the amazing feel of her breaths rushing against my mouth. Seeing the pleasure on her face is my undoing.

I massage her breast while rubbing her clit harder and pushing my finger in deep before curling it.

Brie's back arches and her thighs begin to quiver. Knowing she's close, I keep up the pace. She gasps and then holds her breath as her hips jerk, and then she starts to rub herself against my palm. It strips me bare and fills my chest with an overprotective feeling.

While I watch Brie orgasm, it feels like she's burning an imprint of herself on my soul. I love her with all of my heart. No one will ever compare to her.

Once her body has shuddered through the last of her orgasm, I remove my hands from under her clothes. Pushing an arm under her legs, I lift them over mine, so she's cradled against my chest.

My eyes lock on her blue ones, and the intensity I feel for her overpowers me.

Brie wraps her arms around my neck and hugs me tightly. When she pulls back, I lower my head to hers and press a tender kiss to her mouth.

"I love you, Brie."

A happy smile spreads over her face. "I love you, too."

A matching smile forms on my face, and then I press my mouth to hers, kissing her with everything I feel.

Chapter 27

BRIE

Dear me,

Life is… perfect.

It feels like I've known Colton and Mom forever, and my past is just a distant dream.

I love him so much! And I'm so excited about our future together. We're going to make a difference. I just know it.

B.

Walking into the art class, I go take my seat and open my sketchpad. I'm working on a drawing of how I imagine the art healing center will look.

Once everyone has taken their seats, Miss Snow gets up from behind her desk and says, "I have some good news." She picks up an envelope, then continues, "One of you won the art competition." She waves the envelope in the air, then she gestures in my direction. Like an idiot, I glance at Julie next to me, but then Miss Snow says, "Brie, you won." She claps her hands as I turn my wide gaze back to her.

"Really?" I gasp.

"Yes. Come upfront and claim your prize."

In total shock, I ask, "I won?"

"Yes," she laughs.

I slowly lift my hands to cover my mouth as the realization hits.

Oh my god. I won!

I've never won anything before, and an overwhelming sense of pride begins to fill my chest as I struggle to stand up because my legs feel like Jell-O.

Walking to the front, a smile begins to spread over my face, and my eyes mist up. This is so surreal. Yeah, I did my best, but I didn't think I actually stood a chance.

Miss Snow hands me the envelope, saying, "I'm so proud of you, Brie. Your sketch was amazing, and you deserved to win."

"Thank you." Taking it from her, I hold the envelope to my chest as my smile widens.

Gosh, I'm so happy.

"Open it," Miss Snow encourages me.

My fingers tremble as I tear the side off and pull the paper out. I fold it open, and my eyes dart over the words.

Ahhhhh!!!!

I begin to jump up and down and thrust the paper at Miss Snow. "I got accepted!"

Miss Snow reads the acceptance letter and then gives me such a proud look, it makes emotion well in my throat. "I knew you could do it."

She hands the letter back and I go take my seat again. It's impossible to focus on class because I can't wait to tell Colton. The second the bell rings, I dart out of my chair and wave happily at Miss Snow before rushing out of class.

I run down the hallway, and when I see Colton standing by his locker, I yell, "I won! Colton, I won!" His head snaps in my direction, and he manages to turn toward me just in time as I jump and throw my arms around his neck. "I won the competition," I gasp in his ear. The happiness inside me becomes too much to keep in, and a sob escapes my lips as I whimper, "I got accepted."

Colton holds me tightly and pressing a kiss to my neck, he says, "I told you they'd be crazy not to pick you." When he sets me down on my feet, his hands move up, and he frames my face. "Congrats. I never doubted you'd kick everyone's butt."

Standing on my toes, Colton meets me halfway, and I don't care that we're kissing in the middle of the hallway where everyone can see.

No one else matters.

When we pull away, laughter bubbles over my lips. "I won. I won. I won."

All my excitement makes Colton chuckle, and seeing how happy he is for me only makes me love him more.

———————

Time keeps flying, and I can't believe it's Colton's birthday already. The past month has been incredible.

Luckily his birthday falls on a Friday, and we can spend the entire weekend celebrating it.

I didn't know what to buy him, and instead, I came up with something sentimental. I've just finished writing the last message on a piece of paper and fold it in half before counting all the notes to make sure I have ten. I want to give him one every hour.

Gathering the ones I'll need for school, I neatly tuck them in my pocket and grabbing my bag, I leave my room.

When I walk into the kitchen, Mom's already busy making breakfast, and the smell of bacon hangs in the air.

"Morning." I walk to the coffee pot and pour myself a cup. A wrapped gift on the kitchen table catches my eye. "I can't wait to see what you got him."

She cups her hand by her mouth and whispers, "Books."

Grinning, I reply, "The way to his heart."

Colton comes walking in, asking, "The way to who's heart?"

"Happy birthday," Mom shrieks, and dropping the spatula on the counter, she rushes to give him a hug. "I can't believe my baby's nineteen already. It feels like just yesterday I was still changing your diapers."

I wait for Mom to step back before I hug Colton. I press a quick kiss to his lips, then say, "I hope you'll have a wonderful birthday."

"I'm sure I will," he grins, then he glances at the gift, and he darts over to the table. "Can I open it?"

Mom lets out a burst of laughter and nods.

We watch as Colton tears the paper off, and then the smile on his face broadens as he looks at the books. "I love them." When he gets to the final one, and he opens it, his eyes widen and snap to Mom. "No way! How did you get it signed?" His gaze instantly goes back to the autographed copy of *Between a Rock and a Hard Place* by *Aron Ralston.*

"I ordered it on his website," Mom replies, looking pleased that Colton loves his gift.

"Now, I'm going to reread it." Colton walks to Mom and gives her cheek a kiss. "Thanks, Mom. This is the best gift ever."

I walk to the table and clear the discarded paper before I take the first note out and place it on Colton's plate. Walking to the trashcan, I dump the paper then make Colton a cup of coffee.

"What's this?" I hear Colton ask, and glancing over my shoulder, I watch as he picks up the note. My eyes are glued to him as he reads it, and then the most gorgeous smile spreads over his face.

He glances at me then reads the quote out loud, "You know you're in love when you can't fall asleep because reality is finally better than your dreams. Dr. Seuss," Glancing at Mom, he explains, "I gave Brie quotes of encouragement when we first met."

"Aww..." Mom pulls a cute face, "That's so special."

COLTON

Today is hands down the best birthday ever.

I take my seat in English, and then Brie places another note on my desk. A grin tugs at my mouth as I fold it open.

'Only once in your life, I truly believe, you find someone who can completely turn your world around. You tell them things that you've never shared with another soul, and they absorb everything you say and actually want to hear more. Life seems completely different, exciting, and worthwhile. Your only hope and security is in knowing that they are a part of your life.' – Bob Marley.

I read the quote a couple of times before I turn my gaze to Brie. She smiles at me as I mouth 'Thank You' to her.

Brie could've gotten me anything for my birthday, but these quotes are priceless. It reminds me how far we've come.

Mrs. Ramsey begins with class, and I tuck the note safely into the inside pocket of my jacket.

Throughout the day, Brie keeps dropping one note after the other on my desk, but it's the one in history class that fills me with emotion to the point where I have to swallow hard.

I don't love you because you're the best looking guy in school. I don't love you because you can cook a million times better than me. I don't love you because your kisses are addictive.

I love you because you're my hero.

I love you because no one has a kinder soul, a braver heart, and a stronger mind than you.

I love you, Colton Lawson, because you hear the words, I don't say out loud. You see the tears, I don't cry. Mostly, I love you because you don't push me, you don't lead me – you walk beside me.

xox

B.

Holy shit.

I read the note again, and it fills my heart with so much love for Brie, it's impossible to sit still. Just as Mr. Donati walks into the class, I dart up and press a kiss to Brie's mouth.

I mouth 'Sorry' to Mr. Donati, and he just shakes his head at me with a smile tugging at his mouth.

It's hard to sit through the lesson, and the second the bell rings, I dart up and stare impatiently at Brie as she gathers her stuff. When she's ready, I grab her hand and pull her out of the class.

"Where are we going?" Brie laughs behind me.

"Somewhere more private," I reply, and when we walk around the corner, I drop my bag to the floor. I frame Brie's face with my hands and closing the distance between us with one step, my mouth crashes against hers. I kiss the living hell out of her, wanting her to know how much her words mean to me.

"Let's get it on," Sully belts out as he walks by us, and it makes me pull back.

I watch him walk down the hall before I turn my eyes back to Brie. "Thank you for all the notes. The last one…" I shake my head, "is everything. I love you so much."

Brie steals a quick kiss, and taking my hand, we walk out of the building. "Your birthday's not over yet."

"There are more notes?" I ask, grinning at her.

"Yep."

As we walk to where I parked the truck, we hear a commotion and see Michael and Sully fighting. "Some people will never change."

"Luckily, they're not our problem anymore," Brie mutters, not even glancing at the fight.

"Yeah, you're right."

I open the passenger door for her but instead of getting in, she wraps her arms around my neck. "One last kiss before we head home." She presses her mouth to mine, and the moment our tongues touch, the commotion behind us fades away.

Breaking the kiss, we're both breathless as Brie climbs into the truck. I shut the door and walking around the front, I glance at the fight, just shaking my head.

I slide in behind the steering wheel and start the engine. "It's the weekend," I say, grinning at Brie.

"Finally," she sighs. "This weekend is all about you. I'm even going to attempt to bake you a cake. Mom will supervise, but I can't promise it will be edible."

I let out a chuckle as I steer the truck toward the school gates.

Knowing the weekend lies ahead of us, and I get to spend it with Brie and Mom makes this birthday even better.

The drive home is quick, and walking into the house, a broad smile spreads over my face when I see all the candy and popcorn on the coffee table.

"Go change out of your uniforms so we can start a movie marathon," Mom says, looking excited.

"Please tell me we're not watching romance," I playfully groan.

Mom shakes her head. "Nope, this is your weekend."

"Avengers and Grown Ups?" I ask, feeling hopeful.

"Yes, and anything else you want to watch."

"Yes!" I let out a happy holler. Darting up the stairs, I change into my sweatpants and a t-shirt.

Brie's just as quick cause she's right behind me as we head down the stairs.

I fall down on the couch and let out, "Oomph," as Brie crawls over me to get to her spot.

"Which one first?" Mom asks.

"Grown Ups," I say as I reach for one of the bowls of M&M's. I hold one in front of Brie's mouth, and when her lips part, I drop it inside, then grab a couple for myself.

As the movie begins, the corner of my mouth lifts.

Yeah, life is perfect. I couldn't ask for more.

Chapter 28

Brie

Dear me,

It's Thanksgiving. I've never celebrated it before.

Colton said he's going to show me how to make the perfect turkey. I'll probably end up burning it to a crisp, lol.

This year, I have so much to be thankful for. Colton. Mom. Our lives together. Every day is filled with more love than I could ever imagine experiencing.

It's been just over two months since I moved in with them, and so much has changed. Day's will pass without me thinking about my life before Colton, and even then, it will feel like a bad dream that's fading in and out of my memory.

Yeah, I'm probably suppressing it all. Still, I think, after everything I went through, I deserve to be happy without the constant reminder of what happened. That's the choice

I made. ~~*To just forget.*~~ *I want to forget all my memories before Colton, so I can fill the space with new happy ones.*

Memories of loving Colton and Mom, and of them loving me.

B.

Mom arranged for a photographer to take a family portrait of the three of us last week, and we're supervising while Colton positions the framed picture against the wall in the living room.

"A little to the left," Mom says.

Colton shifts it, and the corner of my mouth twitches when the right side moves up a little.

Mom lets out a chuckle, "An inch down on the right side."

We've been doing this for ten minutes now, and I'm starting to feel sorry for my boyfriend. Walking closer, I help him nudge it up while saying, "Keep the left side like that."

We move it, and Colton let's out a breath of relief, then turning to Mom, he says, "You did that on purpose, right?"

Mom gets an innocent expression on her face while shaking her head. "Who? Me? Never." She lets out a burst of laughter, then teases, "Brie was enjoying watching your butt, and who was I to keep her from enjoying the view."

"I wasn't watching his butt," I laugh.

Mom walks to the kitchen. "Sweetie, you were a second away from drooling."

Colton wags his eyebrows at me and slips his arm around my waist. "Yeah? Did you like the view?"

Giving up, I ask, "Can you blame me?" I let out a dreamy sigh, knowing Mom will get a kick out of it.

I live for moments like this. We're carefree and always laughing. Everything is fun.

"Food," Colton says as he rubs his hands together.

We move to the kitchen, and Colton begins to prep the turkey while Mom turns on the oven so it can warm up. I take my spot by the potatoes and begin to peel them.

After a couple of minutes of work, Mom says, "Want to watch Christmas movies tonight?"

"Don't you think it's a little early? You know it's Thanksgiving today," Colton teases her.

"Then why do they have them on Netflix already?" I ask.

"Exactly," Mom exclaims. "Thanks for backing me, Brie."

"Yup," Colton mutters, "I'll always be out voted when it comes to the two of you."

Mom nudges her shoulder playfully against his. "Aww, you still love us."

The corners of his mouth begin to lift, then he admits, "Yeah, you both have me wrapped around your little fingers."

Wrapping my arm around his lower back, I give him a sideways hug. "We love you too."

When the turkey is roasting in the oven, and there isn't anything else to do, we make ourselves comfortable on the couches.

Colton grabs the remote before Mom can get to it, then says, "If we're watching Christmas movies, we're starting with The Grinch."

"Okay," Mom agrees while shifting into a comfortable position.

"Then Jack Frost," Colton continues.

Mom let's out a burst of laughter. "We can watch whatever you want as long as it's about Christmas."

"Score," Colton chuckles as he presses play.

I haven't watched *The Grinch*, and even though the message is profound, I crack up laughing a couple of times.

COLTON

I carve the turkey, then carry it to the table, saying. "You know we have enough food to feed an army."

"That's the idea," Mom replies. "This better last through to Sunday."

"Yummy." The word bubbles from Brie as she places a big scooping of mashed potatoes on her plate. "Can you pass the gravy?"

I let out a soundless chuckle as I pass it to her and watch as she smothers the mashed potatoes with it.

We all load our plates to the max, then Mom says, "Colton, would you like to start?"

"Sure." I clear my throat as we all take hands. "I'm thankful for my family," I glance between Mom and Brie, "old and new." Keeping my eyes on Brie, I continue, "I'm thankful for the miracle that brought you to us." Her smile widens at my words. "I'm most thankful you gave me a

346

chance." Then I turn my gaze to Mom. "I'm thankful for the best mother in the world."

Mom smiles lovingly. It's her turn, and she first looks at Brie. "I'm thankful for my new daughter. She's everything a mother's heart could ask for." Then Mom looks at me, and her smile wavers before tears begin to well in her eyes. "I'm thankful for the time we had with Brady."

God.

I have to close my eyes for a moment as tears push up my throat.

"I'm thankful for every smile he gave us. For every time I got to hear him laugh."

Fuck.

I can't keep the tears from escaping my eyes and suck in a deep breath of air.

"He'll always be my precious angel."

Brie tightens her hold on my hand, and I'm grateful for the strength she lends me. Clearing my throat, I wait for Mom to continue, "I'm so thankful for you, Colton. You looked after me when I was at my weakest. You never blamed me. You just took over being the parent." She pauses and breathes through the tears as they fall.

My eyes begin to mist up again as I squeeze her hand.

"I'm so honored to be your mother."

347

Her words make emotion well in my chest, and it's hard to keep the tears back, but I manage. Lifting Mom's hand, I press a kiss to the back of it.

When we both look at Brie, tears are streaming down her face, but somehow she's still smiling. "I'm just so thankful for both of you." A sob drifts over her lips, and I tighten my hold on her hand. She focuses on Mom. "I'm thankful to have a mother who loves me."

Yeah, and that's the end of Mom fighting to hold back the tears.

Then Brie locks eyes with me. "I'm eternally thankful that you sat down next to me and dropped a quote on my desk." Brie sucks in a trembling breath. "Thank you for giving me this wonderful life."

I pull my hand free from Mom's and leaning toward Brie, I wrap my arms around her and whisper, "It's only the beginning. I plan on making all your dreams come true."

"You already have," she whispers through her tears.

"Oh, God," Mom complains, "We're going to drown the food."

Pulling away from Brie, I glance at Mom. "You can drown everything except the turkey."

Brie makes a weird sound, something between a sob and laughter.

She wipes her cheeks with the back of her hands, then pops a big bite of mashed potatoes into her mouth. She lets out a delightful groan, mumbling, "Delicious."

In all the time I've known Brie, she has not once complained about anything. Brie relishes in everything that crosses her path.

I take a bite of my mashed potatoes and then understand why Brie groaned. "Mom, this is good. What did you do differently?"

"Way too much cream for my hips to handle," Mom replies.

When we're done stuffing our faces, none of us have the energy to clean up, and just covering the food, we leave it for later.

Lying down on the couch, I open my arms so Brie can get settled against my side. I press play on the next movie but ten minutes into it, Brie's fast asleep. I glance at Mom, and seeing that she's also sleeping, I pause the movie.

Wrapping my arms around Brie, I press a kiss to her hair.

I'm thankful I'm the man who gets to love Brie.

I close my eyes and let out a contented sigh.

Epilogue

BRIE

Colton; 25 & Brie 24

Dear me,

We found the perfect piece of land for the art healing center. It's on the outskirts of town, and it even has a pond with an old oak tree. I want to put a bench beneath the tree.

The opening day is next week. I've never been more excited. I think it will be a peaceful place for people to come and heal.

We have one section for kids and another for adults. Colton, Mom, and I will work with the children. We hired professionals to help counsel the adults. I hope Brady's Haven will make a difference in people's lives.

Well, it's time to leave for work.

TTYL.

B.

I put the finishing touches to the mural of Brady that I painted on the wall at the entrance. It's the first thing everyone will see when they come in.

Standing back, I tilt my head to make sure I didn't miss anything. The corners of my mouth lift as I take in Brady's smile. He looks so much like Colton.

"Wow," Colton murmurs as he comes to stand next to me.

I glance up at him. "Did I capture Brady, right?"

Colton nods, his eyes caressing his brother's features. "It's perfect."

We named the center after Brady, as well. We're hoping to help kids like him.

Glancing around the area, I ask, "Where's Mom?"

"She's placing orders to stock the kitchen." Colton pulls a piece of paper from his pocket and tucks it into mine. "Read that once you've washed your hands."

My eyebrow raises, and I lift my hands. "It's just a little paint."

Chuckling, he walks away. "You have more paint on you than on the wall."

351

My eyes drift over him, taking in the backward baseball cap, the t-shirt stretched over his broad shoulders, and the jeans. *God, those jeans.* "Love the handyman look you've got going," I call after him.

"All for you," he yells back.

I go clean the paint off, and then I pull the paper from my pocket. Opening it, my lips curve up.

'So, I love you because the entire universe conspired to help me find you.' - Paulo Coelho, The Alchemist.

My boyfriend, the romantic.

I tuck the note back in my pocket and walk to the main room to check how the workers are coming along. Glancing around the open space, I notice the easels arrived and go inspect them to make sure they delivered the right ones.

Later, when I'm walking to the kitchen to check on Mom, I grin when Colton comes down the hallway.

"I forgot to tell you they delivered the easels," he mentions before he presses a quick kiss to my lips.

"I saw."

We're just about to pass each other when Colton hands me another note. Taking it, I stare at him as he continues walking. "Did I forget something?" I call out.

"Nope."

Shrugging, I open the piece of paper.

'Once upon a time, there was a boy who loved a girl, and her laughter was a question he wanted to spend his whole life answering.' - Nicole Krauss, The History of Love

This man. God, could I love him more.

Walking into the kitchen, I find Mom checking over a list of cutlery we need. "How are things going in here?"

She glances up. "Good. I think I ordered everything we'll need. When are the two cooks starting again?"

"This coming Thursday."

"Good. Then they can receive the orders." Mom stands up and stretches out. "I'm going to head home. See you later."

"Bye." I look over the list she left on the counter, and wanting to make sure the construction team fixes the cracked tile in the one restroom, I walk out of the kitchen.

Now that everything is almost ready, I can't wait for the opening. We've invited a couple of elite people Colton knows, hoping they'll donate to the worthy cause. He mentioned one of them was Brady's girlfriend.

Glad to see the tile has been replaced, I go search for Colton. When I don't find him, I pull my phone out of my pocket and send him a text.

Me: I'm done for the day. Where are you?

353

Colton: Out by the pond. Come here.

Me: Give me a minute. I just want to lock up the front.

I pull the main doors shut and lock them before I walk to the back of the building. Heading past the patio where we have a firepit, I see Colton standing under the oak tree. When I get closer, a smile forms around my mouth as I notice the blanket spread out over the grass with a picnic basket on top.

"Oooh, I like this," I say when I reach him.

"Yeah? I thought we could celebrate now that all the work is done."

"What about Mom?" I ask as I sit down on the blanket.

There's a light breeze in the air, cooling the air.

"It's just the two of us today." Colton sits down next to me and opens the basket and pulls out a bottle of champagne and two glasses. "Will you pour for us?"

"Sure." My eyes keep darting to all the foods he's unpacking, and I grin when I see the strawberries and cream. "You're in a romantic mood today. What did I do to deserve all this?" I hand one of the flutes with bubbly to him.

"Can't a man just show his woman how much he loves her?" he asks, a secretive look in his eyes.

354

"Yeah, but I get a feeling there's more to this picnic. Did you break something, and this is your way of doing damage control before I find out?"

Colton shakes his head, and then he pulls another folded piece of paper out of his pocket. I watch him take a deep breath, and then he holds it out for me to take.

Opening the page, my eyes slowly drift over the words.

Despite our differences, I fell in love with you. Or maybe it was because of them. It doesn't really matter because with you I've found something rare. You're more than just the love of my life. You're more than my best friend. Every moment we've spent together is imprinted in my heart.

You're my reason for waking up every day. You're my reason to push harder because I want to give you the world. I want to reach for the stars and hand them to you. My whole world fits in your heart.

I'll love you until the sun stops shining, until the moon drops from the night sky, and until the last star has vanished.

Until the world stops turning. Always yours.
Colton.

I stare at the words until they begin to blur, and I don't get any time to try and process what I just read because Colton holds another note out to me.

My eyes dart to his face and seeing how serious he looks, my heart begins to pound in my chest as I take the paper from him.

I suck in a deep breath of air, then open it.

Will you marry me.

Yes. ☐

No. ☐

A sob instantly bursts free from my lips, and I struggle to say, "I don't have a pen."

A pen appears in my line of vision, and I'm a mess as I laugh and cry at the same time. I tick one of the boxes, and wetting my lips, I lift my eyes to Colton's as I hand it back to him.

A smile plays around his mouth, and for a moment, he stares at me before his gaze drops to my answer.

"Thank God." He darts to his feet, pulling me up, and then engulfs me in a hug. "I'm going to make you so happy." Framing my face with his hands, he presses a hard kiss to my lips.

The second he gives me a chance to talk, I say, "You've already made me happy, Colton. So very happy."

COLTON

I pull the engagement ring from my pocket and taking Brie's left hand, I slip it onto her finger. I take a moment to drink in the sight of my ring on her finger, then I lift my eyes to hers. "No pressure, but I want to get married this year."

Brie sputters out a breath of laughter. "You know it's July, right?"

"Yeah?"

She shakes her head, and with a happy smile on her face, she frames my jaw and presses a kiss to my lips, then whispers, "Anything for you."

We sit down again, and my gaze keeps going to her left hand as we pick up the flutes. Brie holds hers in the air. "To us."

I clink mine against hers. "To our happily ever after."

We spend the rest of the afternoon eating while planning our future. There's still so much we want to do. We've just bought a new house closer to the center, and want to renovate it.

"How are the plans coming along for our bedroom and ensuite bathroom?" Brie asks.

"I saw them yesterday. James said he'll submit them for approval by the end of the week." We're breaking down a whole section to build another master bedroom. That way, we'll have our own space, and Mom will have hers.

"Good," Brie murmurs. She glances around, then says, "It's starting to get dark. Should we pack up and head home?"

"Just one more thing." Reaching for her, I pull her closer.

Brie wraps her arms around my neck. "I like where this is going."

Cupping her cheek with my one hand, I stare into her eyes. "I can't wait to change your name to Lawson."

A soft smile forms around her lips. "That makes two of us."

I claim her mouth and express everything I feel as I kiss her. How much I love her. That I can't live without her. She owns every part of my heart and soul.

Breaking the kiss, Brie whispers, "I love you just as much."

I help her up, and we quickly pack up the picnic. Brie takes the blanket while I carry the basket. With our hands interlinked, we walk across the lawn, both our gazes drifting over the dream we created together.

I got my masters in social work, and I'm ready to start helping kids. Brie will focus on helping them express what they feel with art while Mom will take care of the administration side of things.

We're going to make a difference.

The drive home is quick, and when we walk into the house, Mom jumps up from the couch. "Tell me. Tell me. Tell me." And then her eyes fall on Brie's left hand, and she lets out a shriek of happiness. "Let me see!"

"You knew?" Brie laughs as Mom grabs her hand.

"Yeah, but he wouldn't show me the ring," she complains. "It's so beautiful."

Mom finally lets go of Brie's hand, and it gives me the chance to ask, "Did you have dinner?"

"Yeah, I had a chicken and bacon sandwich."

"I'm going to shower. Want to sit out back after I'm done?" I ask as I begin to walk to the stairs.

"I'll pour us coke while the two of you clean up," Mom offers.

Brie follows me to our room, and once we're inside, I say, "I'd ask you to shower with me, but then Mom's going to be waiting a while."

Chuckling, she shakes her head. "We can't have that. You go first."

When we're both finished and dressed in comfortable clothes, we join Mom outside. I stare out over the backyard then say, "Now that the center is done, I need to get to work on the garden."

"We can all do it this weekend," Brie adds.

Mom nods. "I'll plant the flowers."

Her words make the corner of my mouth lift. It's always been her hobby.

My eyes drift from Mom to Brie, and it's during moments like this when we're all relaxed and talking about our future I'm at my happiest.

Just the three of us and endless possibilities.

I reach for Brie's left hand and interweave our fingers. There's a look of contentment on her face as her eyes meet mine. The longer I stare at her, the more I see.

Her wearing a white dress as she walks toward me.

Laughing children.

Crows feet and gray hair.

I see my entire life span out in the blue of her eyes. An endless ocean of happiness.

The End.

If ever life gets too much, please reach out to someone or call a suicide crisis line near you.

List of suicide crisis lines worldwide:

https://en.wikipedia.org/wiki/List_of_suicide_crisis_lines

Black Mountain Academy

Want to read more from Black Mountain Academy?

Drama, angst, love, lust, and everything in-between. Light or dark, twisted or sweet, the BMA series has something for every reader!

Check out the Black Mountain Academy webpage to see all the books available >>> **https://black-mountain-academy.com**

The Heirs

Reading order:

Coldhearted Heir
Novel #1
Hunter Chargill (*Mason and Kingsley's son*)
&
Jade Daniels (*Rhett & Evie's daughter*)

Arrogant Heir
Novel #2
Jase Reyes – (*Julian & Jamie's son*)
&
Mila West – (*Logan & Mia's Daughter*)

Defiant Heir
Novel #3
Kao Reed (*Marcus and Willow's son*)
&
Fallon Reyes (*Falcon & Layla's daughter*)

Loyal Heir
Novel #4
Forest Reyes (*Falcon & Layla's son*)
&
Aria Chargill (*Mason & Kingsley's daughter*)

Callous Heir
Novel #5
Noah West (*Jaxson & Leigh's son*)
&
Carla Reyes (*Julian & Jamie's daughter*)

Trinity Academy

FALCON
Novel #1
Falcon Reyes & Layla Shepard

MASON
Novel #2
Mason Chargill & Kingsley Hunt

LAKE
Novel #3
Lake Cutler & Lee-ann Park

JULIAN
Novel #4
A Stand Alone Novel
Julian Reyes (*Falcon's Brother*)
&
Jamie Truman (*Della's Sister – Heartless, TETLS*)

THE EPILOGUE
A Trinity Academy Novella

Enemies To Lovers

Heartless
Novel #1
Carter Hayes & Della Truman

Reckless
Novel #2
Logan West & Mia Daniels

Careless
Novel #3
Jaxson West & Leigh Baxter

Ruthless
Novel #4
Marcus Reed & Willow Brooks

Shameless
Novel #5
Rhett Daniels & Evie Cole

False Perceptions
Novel #6
A Stand Alone Novel
Hayden Cole *(Evie's Dad)*

Connect with me

Newsletter

FaceBook

Amazon

GoodReads

BookBub

Instagram

Twitter

Website

About the author

Michelle Heard is a Wall Street Journal, and USA Today Bestselling Author who loves creating stories her readers can get lost in. She resides in South Africa with her son where she's always planning her next book to write, and trip to take.

Want to be up to date with what's happening in Michelle's world? Sign up to receive the latest news on her alpha hero releases → NEWSLETTER

If you enjoyed this book or any book, please consider leaving a review. It's appreciated by authors.

Acknowledgments

Brie and Colton took me by surprise. Their story was meant to be a regular high school romance, but when I started writing, they took over. Their voices demanded to be heard. I hope you enjoy their journey as much as I did writing it. Brie and Colton will forever hold a special place in my heart.

Leeann. Girl, you are the golden touch to my words. Thank you for all the plotting, the endless hours of talking things through with me.

Sherrie. Thank you for keeping me sane, my friend. Without you, I'd probably never finish a book.

Allyson, Kelly, Sarah, and Elaine. Thank you for reading everything I write and making sure it all makes sense.

Sheena, without you, there would be tons of plot holes and grammar mistakes for days. Thank you for helping me with the editing.

Candi Kane PR - Thank you for being patient with me and my bad habit of missing deadlines. (I'm finally working on those.)

To my readers, thank you for loving these characters as much as I do.

A special thank you to every blogger and reader who took the time to take part in the cover reveal and release day.

Love ya all tons ;)

Printed in Great Britain
by Amazon

57994747R00210